Men were gathered on the square platform over the smokehold of the House of Absence. They made way for him when he hoisted himself up the ladder. He was wheezing and trembling so that at first he could see nothing. Then he saw. For awhile he forgot everything in the unbelievable sight.

The valley that wound from north to south along the base of Tevar Hill to the river-valley east of the forest was full—full as the river in flood-time, swarming, overrunning with Gaal. They were moving southward, a sluggish, jumbled dark flood, stretching and contracting; always moving moving southward, the Southing.

But in all timepast there had never been a Southing like this. As far as eye could follow up the widening valley northward there were more coming and behind them more, and behind them more.

Beside that slow torrent of people the Winter City of Tevar was nothing—a pebble on the edge of a river in flood. . . .

URSULA KROEBER LE GUIN, daughter of
A. L. Kroeber (anthropologist) and Theodora
Kroeber (author), was born in Berkeley, Cali-
fornia in 1929. She attended college at Radcliffe
and Columbia, and married C. A. LeGuin in
Paris in 1951. The LeGuins and their three
children live in Portland, Oregon.

Ursula LeGuin's other novels include ROCAN-
NON'S WORLD, WIZARD OF EARTHSEA,
CITY OF ILLUSIONS and THE LEFT HAND
OF DARKNESS, all published by Ace Books.
THE LEFT HAND OF DARKNESS in partic-
ular attracted wide attention and strong praise;
it was awarded both the Nebula and the Hugo
Awards.

PLANET

OF

EXILE

BY

URSULA K. LE GUIN

ace books

A Division of Grosset & Dunlap, Inc.
1120 Avenue of the Americas
New York, New York 10036

CHAPTER ONE: *A Handful of Darkness*

IN THE LAST DAYS of the last moonphase of Autumn a wind blew from the northern ranges through the dying forests of Askatevar, a cold wind that smelled of smoke and snow. Slight and shadowy as a wild animal in her light furs, the girl Rolery slipped through the woods, through the storming of dead leaves, away from the walls that stone by stone were rising on the hillside of Tevar and from the busy fields of the last harvest. She went alone and no one called after her. She followed a faint path that led west, scored and rescored in grooves by the passing southward of the footroots, choked in places by fallen trunks or huge drifts of leaves.

Where the path forked at the foot of the Border Ridge she went on straight, but before she had gone ten steps she turned back quickly towards a pulsing rustle that approached from behind.

A runner came down the northward track, bare feet beating in the surf of leaves, the long string that tied his hair whipping behind him. From the north he came at a steady, pounding, lung-bursting pace, and never glanced at Rolery among the trees but pounded past and was gone. The wind blew him on his way to Tevar with his news—storm, disaster, winter, war . . . Incurious, Rolery turned and followed her own evasive path, which zigzagged upward among the great, dead, groaning trunks until at last on the ridge-top she saw sky break clear before her, and beneath the sky the sea.

The dead forest had been cleared from the west face of the ridge. Sitting in the shelter of a huge stump, she could look out on the remote and radiant west, the endless gray reaches of the tidal plain, and, a little below her and to the right, walled and red-roofed on its sea-cliffs, the city of the farborns.

High, bright-painted stone houses jumbled window below window and roof below roof down the slanting cliff-top to the brink. Outside the walls and beneath the cliffs where they ran lower south of the town were miles of pastureland and fields, all dyked and terraced, neat as patterned carpets. From the city wall at the brink of the cliff, over dykes and dunes and straight out over the beach and the slick-shining tidal sands for half a mile, striding on immense arches of stone, a causeway went, linking the city to a strange black island among the sands. A sea-stack, it jutted up black and black-shadowed from the sleek planes and shining levels of the sands, grim rock, obdurate, the top of it arched and towered, a carving more fantastic than even wind or sea could make. Was it a house, a statue, a fort, a funeral cairn? What black skill had hollowed it out and built the incredible bridge, back in timepast when the farborns were mighty and made war? Rolery had never paid much heed to the vague tales of witchcraft that went with mention of the farborns, but now looking at that black place on the sands she saw that it was strange—the first thing truly strange to her that she had ever seen: built in a timepast that had nothing to do with her, by hands that were not kindred flesh and blood, imagined by alien minds. It was sinister, and it drew her. Fascinated, she watched a tiny figure that walked on that high causeway, dwarfed by its great length and height, a little dot or stroke of darkness creeping out to the black towers among the shining sands.

The wind here was less cold; sunlight shone through cloud-rack in the vast west, gliding the streets and roofs below her. The town drew her with its strangeness, and without pausing to summon up courage or decision, reckless, Rolery went lightly and quickly down the mountainside and entered the high gate.

Inside, she walked as light as ever, careless-willful, but that was mostly from pride: her heart beat hard as she followed the gray, perfectly flat stones of the alien street. She glanced from left to right, and right to left, hastily, at the tall houses all built above the ground, with sharp roofs, and windows of transparent stone—so that tale was true! —and at the narrow dirt-lots in front of some houses where bright-leaved kellem and hadun vines, crimson and orange, went climbing up the painted blue or green walls, vivid among all the gray and drab of the autumnal landscape. Near the eastern gate many of the houses stood empty, color stripping and scabbing from the stone, the glittering windows gone. But farther down the streets and steps the houses were lived in, and she began to pass farborns in the street.

They looked at her. She had heard that farborns would meet one's eyes straight on, but did not put the story to test. At least none of them stopped her; her clothing was not unlike theirs, and some of them, she saw in her quick flicking glances, were not very much darker-skinned than men. But in the faces that she did not look at she sensed the unearthly darkness of the eyes.

All at once the street she walked on ended in a broad open place, spacious and level, all gold-and-shadow-streaked by the westering sun. Four houses stood about this square, houses the size of little hills, fronted with great rows of arches and above these with alternate gray and transparent stones. Only four streets led into this square and each could be shut with a gate that swung from the walls of the four great houses; so the square was a fort

within a fort or a town within a town. Above it all a piece
of one building stuck straight up into the air and towered
there, bright with sunlight.

It was a mighty place, but almost empty of people.

In one sandy corner of the square, itself large as a field,
a few farborn boys were playing. Two youths were having
a fierce and skillful wrestling match, and a bunch of younger boys in padded coats and caps were as fiercely practic-
ing cut-and-thrust with wood swords. The wrestlers were
wonderful to watch, weaving a slow dangerous dance about
each other, then engaging with deft and sudden grace.
Along with a couple of farborns, tall and silent in their
furs, Rolery stood looking on. When all at once the bigger
wrestler went sailing head over heels to land flat on his
brawny back she gave a gasp that coincided with his, and
then laughed with surprise and admiration. "Good throw,
Jonkendy!" a farborn near her called out, and a woman
on the far side of the arena clapped her hands. Oblivious,
absorbed, the younger boys fought on, thrusting and
whacking and parrying.

She had not known the witchfolk bred up warriors, or
prized strength and skill. Though she had heard of their
wrestling, she had always vaguely imagined them as
hunched back and spiderlike in a gloomy den over a pot-
ter's wheel, making the delicate bits of pottery and clear-
stone that found their way into the tents of mankind. And
there were stories and rumors and scraps of tales; a hunter
was "lucky as a farborn"; a certain kind of earth was called
witch-ore because the witchfolk prized it and would trade
for it. But scraps were all she knew. Since long before her
birth the Men of Askatevar had roamed in the east and
north of their range. She had never come with a harvest-
load to the storerooms under Tevar Hill, so she had never
been on this western border at all till this moonphase,
when all the Men of the Range of Askatever came together with their flocks and families to build the Winter
City over the buried granaries. She knew nothing, really,

about the alien race, and when she became aware that the winning wrestler, the slender youth called Jonkendy, was staring straight into her face, she turned her head away and drew back in fear and distaste.

He came up to her, his naked body shining black with sweat. "You come from Tevar, don't you?" he asked, in human speech, but sounding half the words wrong. Happy with his victory, brushing sand off his lithe arms, he smiled at her.

"Yes."

"What can we do for you here? Anything you want?"

She could not look at him from so close, of course, but his tone was both friendly and mocking. It was a boyish voice; she thought he was probably younger than she. She would not be mocked. "Yes," she said coolly. "I want to see that black rock on the sands."

"Go on out. The causeway's open."

He seemed to be trying to peer into her lowered face. She turned further from him.

"If anybody stops you, tell them Jonkendy Li sent you," he said, "or should I go with you?"

She would not even reply to this. Head high and gaze down she headed for the street that led from the square towards the causeway. None of these grinning black falsemen would dare think she was afraid . . .

Nobody followed. Nobody seemed to notice her, passing her in the short street. She came to the great pillars of the causeway, glanced behind her, looked ahead and stopped.

The bridge was immense, a road for giants. From up on the ridge it had looked fragile, spanning fields and dunes and sand with the light rhythm of its arches; but here she saw that it was wide enough for twenty men to walk abreast on, and led straight to the looming black gates of the towerrock. No rail divided the great walkway from the gulf of air. The idea of walking out on it was simply wrong. She could not do it; it was not a walk for human feet.

A sidestreet led her to a western gate in the city wall. She hurried past long, empty pens and byres and slipped out the gate, intending to go on round the walls and be off home.

But here where the cliffs ran lower, with many stairs cut in them, the fields below lay peaceful and patterned in the yellow afternoon; and just across the dunes lay the wide beach, where she might find the long green seaflowers that women of Askatevar kept in their chests and on feastdays wreathed in their hair. She smelled the queer smell of the sea. She had never walked on the sea-sands in her life. The sun was not low yet. She went down a cliff stairway and through the fields, over the dykes and dunes and ran out at last onto the flat and shining sands that went on and on out of sight to the north and west and south.

Wind blew, faint sun shone. Very far ahead in the west she heard an unceasing sound, an immense, remote voice murmuring, lulling. Firm and level and endless, the sand lay under her feet. She ran for the joy of running, stopped and looked with a laugh of exhilaration at the causeway arches marching solemn and huge beside the tiny wavering line of her footprints, ran on again and stopped again to pick up silvery shells that lay half buried in the sand. Bright as a handful of colored pebbles the farborn town perched on the cliff-top behind her. Before she was tired of salt wind and space and solitude, she was out almost as far as the towerrock, which now loomed dense black between her and the sun.

Cold lurked in that long shadow. She shivered and set off running again to get out of the shadow, keeping a good long ways from the black bulk of rock. She wanted to see how low the sun was getting, how far she must run to see the first waves of the sea.

Faint and deep on the wind a voice rang in her ears, calling something, calling so strangely and urgently that she stopped still and looked back with a qualm of dread at the great black island rising up out of the sand. Was the witchplace calling to her?

On the unrailed causeway, over one of the piers that stuck down into the island rock, high and distant up there, a black figure stood calling to her.

She turned and ran, then stopped and turned back. Terror grew in her. Now she wanted to run, and did not. The terror overcame her and she could not move hand or foot but stood shaking, a roaring in her ears. The witch of the black tower was weaving his spider-spell about her. Flinging out his arms he called again the piercing urgent words she did not understand, faint on the wind as a seabird's call, *staak, staak!* The roaring in her ears grew and she cowered down on the sand.

Then all at once, clear and quiet inside her head, a voice said, "Run. Get up and run. To the island—now, quick." And before she knew, she had got to her feet; she was running. The quiet voice spoke again to guide her. Unseeing, sobbing for breath, she reached black stairs cut in the rock and began to struggle up them. At a turning a black figure ran to meet her. She reached up her hand and was half led, half dragged, up one more staircase, then released. She fell against the wall, for her legs would not hold her. The black figure caught her, helped her stand, and spoke aloud in the voice that had spoken inside her skull: "Look," he said, "there it comes."

Water crashed and boiled below them with a roar that shook the solid rock. The waters parted by the island joined white and roaring, swept on, hissed and foamed and crashed on the long slope to the dunes, stilled to a rocking of bright waves.

Rolery stood clinging to the wall, shaking. She could not stop shaking.

"The tide comes in here just a bit faster than a man can run," the quiet voice behind her said. "And when it's in, it's about twenty feet deep here around the Stack. Come on up this way . . . That's why we lived out here in the old days, you see. Half of the time it's an island. Used to lure an enemy army out onto the sands just before the tide came in, if they didn't know much about the tides . . . Are you all right?"

Rolery shrugged slightly. He did not seem to understand the gesture, so she said, "Yes." She could understand his speech, but he used a good many words she had never heard, and pronounced most of the rest wrong.

"You come from Tevar?"

She shrugged again. She felt sick and wanted to cry, but did not. Climbing the next flight of stairs cut in the black rock, she put her hair straight, and from its shelter glanced up for a split second sideways at the farborn's face. It was strong, rough, and dark, with grim, bright eyes, the dark eyes of the alien.

"What were you doing on the sands? Didn't anyone warn you about the tide?"

"I didn't know," she whispered.

"Your Elders know. Or they used to last Spring when your tribe was living along the coast here. Men have damn short memories." What he said was harsh, but his voice was always quiet and without harshness. "This way now. Don't worry—the whole place is empty. It's been a long time one of you people set foot on the Stack . . ."

They had entered a dark door and tunnel and come out into a room which she thought huge till they entered the next one. They passed through gates and courts open to the sky, along arched galleries that leaned far out above the sea, through rooms and vaulted halls, all silent, empty, dwelling places of the sea-wind. The sea rocked its wrinkled silver far below now. She felt light-headed, insubstantial.

"Does nobody live here?" she asked in a small voice.

"Not now."

"It's your Winter City?"

"No, we winter in the town. This was built as a fort. We

had a lot of enemies in the old Years . . . Why were you on the sands?"

"I wanted to see . . ."

"See what?"

"The sands. The ocean. I was in your town first, I wanted to see . . ."

"All right! No harm in that." He led her through a gallery so high it made her dizzy. Through the tall, pointed arches crying seabirds flew. Then passing down a last narrow corridor they came out under a gate, and crossed a clanging bridge of swordmetal onto the causeway.

They walked between tower and town, between sky and sea, in silence, the wind pushing them always towards the right. Rolery was cold, and unnerved by the height and strangeness of the walk, by the presence of the dark falseman beside her, walking with her pace for pace.

As they entered the town he said abruptly, "I won't mind-speak you again. I had to then."

"When you said to run—" she began, then hesitated, not sure what he was talking about, or what had happened out on the sands.

"I thought you were one of us," he said as if angry, and then controlled himself. "I couldn't stand and watch you drown. Even if you deserved to. But don't worry. I won't do it again, and it didn't give me any power over you. No matter what your Elders may tell you. So go on, you're free as air and ignorant as ever."

His harshness was real, and it frightened Rolery. Impatient with her fear she inquired, shakily but with impudence, "Am I also free to come back?"

At that the farborn looked at her. She was aware, though she could not look up at his face, that his expression had changed. "Yes. You are. May I know your name, daughter of Askatevar?"

"Rolery of Wold's Kin."

"Wold's your grandfather?—your father? He's still alive?"

13

"Wold closes the circle in the Stone Pounding," she said loftily, trying to assert herself against his air of absolute authority. How could a farborn, a false-man, kinless and beneath law, be so grim and lordly?

"Give him greeting from Jakob Agat Alterra. Tell him that I'll come to Tevar tomorrow to speak to him. Farewell, Rolery." And he put out his hand in the salute of equals so that without thinking she did the same, laying her open palm against his.

Then she turned and hurried up the steep streets and steps, drawing her fur hood up over her head, turning from the few farborns she passed. Why did they stare in one's face so, like corpses or fish? Warm-blooded animals and human beings did not go staring in one another's eyes that way. She came out of the landward gate with a great sense of relief, and made her quick way up the ridge in the last reddish sunlight, down through the dying woods, and along the path leading to Tevar. As twilight verged into darkness, she saw across the stubble-fields little stars of fire light from the tents encircling the unfinished Winter City on the hill. She hurried on towards warmth and dinner and humankind. But even in the big sister-tent of her Kin, kneeling by the fire and stuffing herself with stew among the womenfolk and children, still she felt a strangeness lingering in her mind. Closing her right hand, she seemed to hold against her palm a handful of darkness, where his touch had been.

CHAPTER TWO: *In the Red Tent*

"THIS SLOP'S COLD," he growled, pushing it away. Then seeing old Kerly's patient look as she took the bowl to reheat it, he called himself a cross old fool. But none of his wives—he had only one left—none of his daughters, none of the women could cook up a bowl of bhan-meal the way Shakatany had done. What a cook she had been, and young . . . his last young wife. And she had died, out there in the eastern range, died young while he went on living and living, waiting for the bitter Winter to come.

A girl came by in a leather tunic stamped with the trifoliate mark of his Kin, a granddaughter probably. She looked a little like Shakatany. He spoke to her, though he did not remember her name. "Was it you that came in late last night, kinswoman?"

He recognized the turn of her head and smile. She was the one he teased, the one that was indolent, impudent, sweet-natured, solitary; the child born out of season. What the devil was her name?"

"I bring you a message, Eldest."

"Whose message?"

"He called himself by a big name—Jakat-abat-bolterra? I can't remember it all."

"Alterra? That's what the farborns call their chiefs. Where did you see this man?"

15

"It wasn't a man, Eldest, it was a farborn. He sent greetings, and a message that he'll come today to Tevar to speak to the Eldest."

"Did he, now?" said Wold, nodding a little, admiring her effrontery. "And you're his message-bearer?"

"He chanced to speak to me . . ."

"Yes, yes. Did you know, kinswoman, that among the Men of Pernmek Range an unwed woman who speaks to a farborn is . . . punished?"

"Punished how?"

"Never mind."

"The Pernmek men are a lot of kloob-eaters, and they shave their heads. What do they know about farborns, anyway? They never come to the coast. . . . I heard once in some tent that the Eldest of my Kin had a farborn wife. In other days."

"That was true. In other days." The girl waited, and Wold looked back, far back into another time: timepast, the Spring. Colors, fragrances long faded, flowers that had not bloomed for forty moonphases, the almost forgotten sound of a voice . . . "She was young. She died young. Before Summer ever came." After a while he added, "Besides, that's not the same as an unwed girl speaking to a farborn. There's a difference, kinswoman."

"Why so?"

Though impertinent, she deserved an answer. "There are several reasons, and some are better than others. This mainly: a farborn takes only one wife, so a true-woman marrying him would bear no sons."

"Why would she not, Eldest?"

"Don't women talk in the sister-tent any more? Are you all so ignorant? Because human and farborn can't conceive together! Did you never hear of that? Either a sterile mating or else miscarriages, misformed monsters that don't come to term. My wife, Arilia, who was farborn, died in miscarrying a child. Her people have no rule; their women are like men, they marry whom they like. But among Man-

16

kind there is law: women lie with human men, marry human men, bear human children!"

She looked a little sick and sorry. Presently, looking off at the scurry and bustle on the walls of the Winter City, she said, "A fine law for women who have men to lie with . . ."

She looked to be about twenty moonphases old, which meant she was the one born out of season, right in the middle of the Summer Fallow when children were not born. The sons of Spring would by now be twice or three times her age, married, remarried, prolific; the Fall-born were all children yet. But some Spring-born fellow would take her for third or fourth wife; there was no need for her to complain. Perhaps he could arrange a marriage for her, though that depended on her affiliations. "Who is your mother, kinswoman?"

She looked straight at his belt-clasp and said, "Shakatany was my mother. Have you forgotten her?"

"No, Rolery," he replied after a little while. "I haven't. Listen now, daughter, where did you speak to this Alterra? Was his name Agat?"

"That was part of his name."

"So I knew his father and his father's father. He is of the kin of the woman . . . the farborn we spoke of. He would be perhaps his sister's son or brother's son."

"Your nephew then. My cousin," said the girl, and gave a sudden laugh. Wold also grinned at the grotesque logic of this affiliation.

"I met him when I went to look at the ocean," she explained, "there on the sands. Before I saw a runner coming from the north. None of the women know. Was there news Is the Southing going to begin?"

"Maybe, maybe," said Wold. He had forgotten her name again. "Run along, child, help your sisters in the fields there," he said, and forgetting her, and the bowl of bhan he had been waiting for, he got up heavily and went round his great red-painted tent to gaze at the swarming workers on the earth-houses and the walls of the Winter City, and beyond them to the north. The northern sky this morning was very blue, clear, cold, over bare hills.

Vividly he remembered the life in those peak-roofed warrens dug into the earth: the huddled bodies of a hundred sleepers, the old women waking and lighting the fires that sent heat and smoke into all his pores, the smell of boiling wintergrass, the noise, the stink, the close warmth of winter in those burrows under the frozen ground. And the cold cleanly stillness of the world above, wind-scoured or snow-covered, when he and the other young hunters ranged far from Tevar hunting the snowbirds and korio and the fat wespries that followed the frozen rivers down from the remotest north. And over there, right across the valley, from a patch of snowcrop there had risen up the lolling white head of a snowghoul. . . . And before then, before the snow and ice and white beasts of Winter, there had once before been bright weather like this: a bright day of golden wind and blue sky, cold above the hills. And he, no man, only a brat among the brats and women, looking up at flat white faces, red plumes, capes of queer, feathery grayish fur; voices had barked like beasts in words he did not understand, while the men of his Kin and the Elders of Askatevar had answered in stern voices, bidding the flat-faces go on. And before that there had been a man who came running from the north with the side of his face burnt and bloody, crying, "The Gaal, the Gaal! They came through our camp at Pekna! . . ."

Clearer than any present voice he heard that hoarse shout ring across his lifetime, the sixty moonphases that lay between him and that staring, listening brat, between this bright day and that bright day. Where was Pekna? Lost under the rains, the snows; and the thaws of Spring had washed away the bones of the massacred, the rotted tents, the memory, the name.

There would be no massacres this time when the Gaal came south through the Range of Askatevar. He had seen to that. There was some good in outliving your time and remembering old evils. Not one clan or family of the Men of all this Range was left out in the Summerlands to be caught unawares by the Gaal or the first blizzard. They were all here. Twenty hundreds of them, with the little Fall-borns thick as leaves skipping about under your feet, and women chattering and gleaning in the fields like flocks of migratory birds, and men swarming to build up the houses and walls of the Winter City with the old stones on the old foundations, to hunt the last of the migrant beasts, to cut and store endless wood from the forests and peat from the Dry Bog, to round up and settle the hann in great byres and feed them until the wintergrass should begin to grow. All of them, in this labor that had gone on half a moonphase now, had obeyed him, and he had obeyed the old Way of Man. When the Gaal came they would shut the city gates; when the blizzards came they would shut the earth-house doors, and they would survive till Spring. They would survive.

He sat down on the ground behind his tent, lowering himself heavily, sticking out his gnarled, scarred legs into the sunlight. Small and whitish the sun looked, though the sky was flawlessly clear; it seemed half the size of the great sun of Summer, smaller even than the moon. "Sun shrunk to moon, cold comes soon . . ." The ground was damp with the long rains that had plagued them all this moonphase, and scored here and there with the little ruts left by the migrating footroots. What was it the girl had asked him—about farborns, about the runner, that was it. The fellow had come panting in yesterday—was it yesterday?—with a tale of the Gaal attacking the Winter City of Tlokna, up north there near the Green Mountains. There was lie or panic in that tale. The Gaal never attacked stone walls. Flat-nosed barbarians, in their plumes and dirt, running southward like homelsss animals at the approach of Winter—they couldn't take a city. And anyway, Pekna was only a little hunting camp, not a walled city. The runner lied. It was all right. They would survive. Where was

19

the fool woman with his breakfast? Here, now, it was warm, here in the sun . . .

Wold's eighth wife crept up with a basket of steaming bhan, saw he was asleep, sighed grumpily, and crept away again to the cooking-fire.

That afternoon when the farborn came to his tent, dour guards around him and a ragtag of leering, jeering children trailing behind, Wold remembered what the girl had said, laughing: "Your nephew, my cousin." So he heaved himself up and stood to greet the farborn with averted face and hand held out in the greeting of equals.

As an equal the alien greeted him, unhesitating. They had always that arrogance, that air of thinking themselves as good as men, whether or not they really believed it. This fellow was tall, well-made, still young; he walked like a chief. Except for his darkness and his dark, unearthly eyes, he might have been thought to be human.

"I am Jakob Agat, Eldest."

"Be welcòme in my tent and the tents of my Kin, Alterra."

"I hear with my heart," the farborn said, making Wold grin a little; he had not heard anybody say that since his father's time. It was strange how farborns always remembered old ways, digging up things buried in timepast. How could this young fellow know a phrase that only Wold and perhaps a couple of the other oldest men of Tevar remembered? It was part of the farborns' strangeness, which was called witchery, and which made people fear the dark folk. But Wold had never feared them.

"A noblewoman of your Kin dwelt in my tents, and I walked in the streets of your city many times in Spring. I remember this. So I say that no man of Tevar will break the peace between our people while I live."

"No man of Landin will break it while I live."

The old chief had been moved by his little speech as he made it; there were tears in his eyes, and he sat down on his chest of painted hide clearing his throat and blinking.

Agat stood erect, black-cloaked, dark eyes in a dark face. The young hunters who guarded him fidgeted, children peered whispering and shoving in the open side of the tent. With one gesture Wold blew them all away. The tentside was lowered, old Kerly lit the tentfire and scurried out again, and he was alone with the alien. "Sit down," he said. Agat did not sit down. He said, "I listen," and stood there. If Wold did not ask him to be seated in front of the other humans, he would not be seated when there were none to see. Wold did not think all this nor decide upon it, he merely sensed it through a skin made sensitive by a long lifetime of leading and controlling people.

He sighed and said, "Wife!" in his cracked bass voice. Old Kerly reappeared, staring. "Sit down," Wold said to Agat, who sat down crosslegged by the fire. "Go away," Wold growled to his wife, who vanished.

Silence. Elaborately and laboriously, Wold undid the fastenings of a small leather bag that hung from the waist-strap of his tunic, extracted a tiny lump of solidified gesin-oil, broke from it a still tinier scrap, replaced the lump, re-tied the bag, and laid the scrap on a hot coal at the edge of the fire. A little curl of bitter greenish smoke went up; Wold and the alien both inhaled deeply and closed their eyes. Wold leaned back against the big pitch-coated urine basket and said, "I listen."

"Eldest, we have had news from the north."

"So have we. There was a runner yesterday." Was it yesterday?"

"Did he speak of the Winter City at Tlokna?"

The old man sat looking into a fire a while, breathing deep as if to get a last whiff of the gesin, chewing the inside of his lips, his face (as he well knew) dull as a piece of wood, blank, senile.

"I'd rather not be the bearer of ill news," the alien said in his quiet, grave voice.

"You aren't. We've heard it already. It is very hard. Alterra, to know the truth in stories that come from far away,

21

from other tribes in other ranges. It's eight days' journey even for a runner from Tlokna to Tevar, twice that long with tents and hann. Who knows? The gates of Tevar will be ready to shut, when the Southing comes by. And you in your city that you never leave, surely your gates need no mending?"

"Eldest, it will take very strong gates this time. Tlonka had walls, and gates, and warriors. Now it has none. This is no rumor. Men of Landin were there, ten days ago; they've been watching the borders for the first Gaal. But the Gaal are coming all at once—"

"Alterra, I listen . . . Now you listen. Men sometimes get frightened and run away before the enemy ever comes. We hear this tale and that tale too. But I am old. I have seen autumn twice, I have seen Winter come, I have seen the Gaal come south. I will tell you the truth."

"I listen," the alien said.

"The Gaal live in the north beyond the farthest ranges of men who speak our language. They have great grassy Summerlands there, so the story says, beneath mountains that have rivers of ice on their tops. After Mid-Autumn the cold and the beasts of the snow begin to come down into their lands from the farthest north where it is always Winter, and like our beasts the Gaal move south. They bring their tents, but build no cities and save no grain. They come through Tevar Range while the stars of the Tree are rising at sunset and before the Snowstar rises, at the turn from Fall to Winter. If they find families traveling unprotected, hunting camps, unguarded flocks or fields, they'll kill and steal. If they see a Winter City standing built, and warriors on its walls, they go by waving their spears and yelling, and we shoot a few darts into the backsides of the last ones. . . . They go on and on, and stop only somewhere far south of here; some men say it's warmer where they spend the Winter—who knows? But that is the Southing. I know. I've seen it, Alterra, and seen them return north again in the thaws when the forests are growing. They don't attack stone cities. They're like water, water running and noisy, but the stone divides it and is not moved. Tevar is stone."

The young farborn sat with bowed head, thinking, long enough that Wold could glance directly at his face for a moment.

"All you say, Eldest, is truth, entire truth, and has always been true in past Years. But this is . . . a new time . . . I am a leader among my people, as you are of yours. I come as one chief to another, seeking help. Believe me—listen to me, our people must help each other. There is a great man among the Gaal, a leader, they call him Kubban or Kobban. He has united all their tribes and made an army of them. The Gaal aren't stealing stray hann along their way, they're besieging and capturing the Winter Cities in all the Ranges along the coast, killing the Spring-born men, enslaving the women, leaving Gaal warriors in each city to hold and rule it over the Winter. Come Spring, when the Gaal come north again, they'll stay; these lands will be their lands—these forests and fields and Summerlands and cities and all their people—what's left of them . . ."

The old man stared aside a while and then said very heavily, in anger, "You talk, I don't listen. You say my people will be beaten, killed, enslaved. My people are men and you're a farborn. Keep your black talk for your own black fate!"

"If men are in danger, we're in worse danger. Do you know how many of us there are in Landin now, Eldest? Less than two thousand."

"So few? What of the other towns? Your people lived on the coast to the north, when I was young."

"Gone. The survivors came to us."

"War? Sickness? You have no sickness, you farborns."

"It's hard to survive on a world you weren't made for," Agat said with grim brevity. "At any rate we're few, we're weak in numbers: we ask to be the allies of Tevar when the Gaal come. And they'll come within thirty days."

"Sooner than that, if there are Gaal at Tlonka now.

They're late already, the snow will fall any day. They'll be hurrying."

"They're not hurrying, Eldest. They're coming slowly because they're coming all together—fifty, sixty, seventy thousand of them!"

Suddenly and most horribly, Wold saw what he said: saw the endless horde filing rank behind rank through the moun tain passes, led by a tall slab-faced chief, saw the men of Tlonka—or was it of Tevar?—lying slaughtered under the broken walls of their city, ice forming in splinters over pud-dled blood. . . . He shook his head to clear out these vis-ions. What had come over him? He sat silent a while chewing the inside of his lips.

"Well, I have heard you, Alterra."

"Not entirely, Eldest." This was barbarian rudeness, but the fellow was an alien, and after all a chief of his own kind. Wold let him go ahead. "We have time to prepare. If the men of Askatevar and the men of Allakskat and of Pern-mek will make alliance, and accept our help, we can make an army of our own. If we wait in force, ready for the Gaal, on the north border of your three Ranges, then the whole Southing rather than face that much strength might turn aside and go down the mountain trails to the east. Twice in earlier Years our records say they took that eastern way. Since it's late and getting colder, and there's not much game left, the Gaal may turn aside and hurry on if they meet men ready to fight. My guess is that Kubban has no real tactic other than surprise and multitude. We can turn him."

"The men of Pernmek and Allakskat are in their Winter Cities now, like us. Don't you know the Way of Men yet? There are no battles fought in Winter!"

"Tell that law to the Gaal, Eldest! Take your own counsel, but believe my words!" The farborn rose, impelled to his feet by the intensity of his pleading and warning. Wold felt sorry for him, as he often did for young men, who have not seen how passion and plan over and over are wasted, how their lives and acts are wasted between desire and fear.

"I have heard you," he said with stolid kindliness. "The Elders of my people will hear what you've said."

"Then may I come tomorrow to hear—"

"Tomorrow, next day . . ."

"Thirty days, Eldest! Thirty days at most!"

"Alterra, the Gaal will come, and will go. The Winter will come and will not go. What good for a victorious warrior to return to an unfinished house, when the earth turns to ice? When we're ready for Winter we'll worry about the Gaal. . . . Now sit down again." He dug into his pouch again for a second bit of gesin for their closing whiff. "Was your father Agat also? I knew him when he was young. And one of my worthless daughters told me that she met you while she was walking on the sands."

The farborn looked up rather quickly, and then said, "Yes, so we met. On the sands between tides."

CHAPTER THREE: *The True Name of the Sun*

WHAT CAUSED the tides along this coast, the great diurnal swinging in and swinging out of fifteen to fifty feet of water? Not one of the Elders of the City of Tevar could answer that question. Any child in Landin could: the moon caused the tides, the pull of the moon. . . .

And moon and earth circled each other, a stately circle taking four hundred days to complete, a moonphase. And together the double planet circled the sun, a great and solemnly whirling dance in the midst of nothingness. Sixty moonphases that dance lasted, twenty-four thousand days, a lifetime, a Year. And the name of the center and sun— the name of the sun was Eltanin: Gamma Draconis.

Before he entered under the gray branches of the forest, Jakob Agat looked up at the sun sinking into a haze above the western ridge and in his mind called it by its true name, the meaning of which was that it was not simply the Sun, but a sun: a star among the stars.

The voice of a child at play rang out behind him on the slopes of Tevar Hill, recalling to him the jeering, sidelong-looking faces, the mocking whispers that hid fear, the yells behind his back—"There's a farborn here! Come and look at him!" Agat, alone under the trees, walked faster, trying to outwalk humiliation. He had been humiliated among the tents ot Tevar and had suffered also from the sense of isolation. Having lived all his life in a little community of his own kind, knowing every name and face and heart, it was hard for him to face strangers. Especially hostile strangers of a different species, in crowds, on their own ground. The fear and humiliation now caught up with him so that he stopped walking altogether for a moment. *I'll be damned if I'll go back there!* he thought. *Let the old fool have his way, and sit smoke-drying himself in his stinking tent till the Gaal come. Ignorant, bigoted, quarrelsome, mealy-face, yellow-eyed barbarians, wood-headed hilfs, let 'em all burn!*

"Alterra?"

The girl had come after him. She stood a few yards behind him on the path, her hand on the striated white trunk of a basuk tree. Yellow eyes blazed with excitement and mockery in the even white of her face. Agat stood motionless.

"Alterra?" she said again in her light, sweet voice, looking aside.

"What do you want?"

She drew back a bit. "I'm Rolery," she said. "On the sands—"

"I know who you are. Do you know who I am? I'm a falseman, a farborn. If your tribesmen see you with me they'll either castrate me or ceremonially rape you—I don't know which rules you follow. Now go home!"

"My people don't do that. And there is kinship between you and me," she said, her tone stubborn but uncertain.

He turned to go.

"Your mother's sister died in our tents—"

"To our shame," he said, and went on. She did not follow.

He stopped and looked back when he took the left fork up the ridge. Nothing stirred in all the dying forest, except one belated footroot down among the dead leaves, creeping with its excruciating vegetable obstinacy southward, leaving a thin track scored behind it.

Racial pride forbade him to feel any shame for his treat-

27

ment of the girl, and in fact he felt relief and a return of confidence. He would have to get used to the hilfs' insults and ignore their bigotry. They couldn't help it; it was their own kind of obstinacy, it was their nature. The old chief had shown, by his own lights, real courtesy and patience. He, Jakob Agat, must be equally patient, and equally obstinate. For the fate of his people, the life of mankind on this world, depended on what these hilf tribes did and did not do in the next thirty days. Before the crescent moon rose, the history of a race for six hundred moonphases, ten Years, twenty generations, the long struggle, the long pull might end. Unless he had luck, unless he had patience.

Dry leafless, with rotten branches, huge trees stood crowded and aisled for miles along these hills, their roots withered in the earth. They were ready to fall under the push of the north wind, to lie under frost and snow for thousands of days and nights, to rot in the long, long thaws of Spring, to enrich with their vast death the earth where, very deep, very deeply sleeping, their seeds lay buried now. Patience, patience . . .

In the wind he came down the bright stone streets of Landin to the Square, and passing the school-children at their exercises in the arena, entered the arcaded, towered building that was called by an old name: the Hall of the League.

Like the other buildings around the Square, it had been built five years ago when Landin was the capital of a strong and flourishing little nation, the time of strength. The whole first floor was a spacious meeting-hall. All around its gray walls were broad, delicate designs picked out in gold. On the east wall a stylized sun surrounded by nine planets faced the west wall's pattern of seven planets in very long ellipses round their sun. The third planet of each system was double, and set with crystal. Above the doors and at the far end, round dial-faces with fragile and ornate hands told that this present day was the 391st day of the 45th moonphase of the Tenth Local Year of the Colony on Gamma Draconis III. They also told that it was the two hundred and second day of Year 1405 of the League of All Worlds; and that it was the twelfth of August at home.

Most people doubted that there was still a League of All Worlds, and a few paradoxicalists liked to question whether there ever had in fact been a home. But the clocks, here in the Great Assembly and down in the Records Room underground, which had been kept running for six hundred League Years, seemed to indicate by their origin and their steadfastness that there had been a League and that there still was a home, a birthplace of the race of man. Patiently they kept the hours of a planet lost in the abyss of darkness and years. Patience, patience . . .

The other Alterrans were waiting for him in the library upstairs, or came in soon, gathering around the driftwood fire on the hearth: ten of them all together. Seiko and Alla Pasfal lighted the gas jets and turned them low. Though Agat had said nothing at all, his friend Huru Pilotson coming to stand beside him at the fire said, "Don't let 'em get you, Jakob. A herd of stupid stubborn nomads—they'll never learn."

"Have I been sending?"

"No, of course not." Huru giggled. He was a quick, slight, shy fellow, devoted to Jakob Agat. That he was a homosexual and that Agat was not was a fact well-known to them both, to everybody around them, to everyone in Landin indeed. Everybody in Landin knew everything, and candor, though wearing and difficult, was the only possible solution to this problem of over-communication.

"You expected too much when you left, that's all. Your disappointment shows. But don't let 'em get you, Jakob. They're just hilfs."

Seeing the others were listening, Agat said aloud, "I told the old man what I'd planned to; he said he'd tell their Council. How much he understood and how much he believed, I don't know."

"If he listened at all it's better than I'd hoped," said Alla

Pasfal, sharp and frail, with blueblack skin, and white hair crowning her worn face. "Wold's been around as long as I have—longer. Don't expect him to welcome wars and changes."

"But he should be well disposed—he married a human," Dermat said.

"Yes, my cousin Arilia, Jakob's aunt—the exotic one in Wold's female zoo. I remember the courtship," Alla Pasfal said with such bitter sarcasm that Dermat wilted.

"He didn't make any decision about helping us? Did you tell him your plan about going up to the border to meet the Gaal?" Jonkendy Li stammered, hasty and disappointed. He was very young, and had been hoping for a fine war with marchings-forth and trumpets. So had they all. It beat being starved to death or burned alive.

"Give them time. They'll decide," Agat said gravely to the boy.

"How did Wold receive you?" asked Seiko Esmit. She was the last of a great family. Only the sons of the first leader of the Colony had borne that name Esmit. With her it would die. She was Agat's age, a beautiful and delicate woman, nervous, rancorous, repressed. When the Alterrans met, her eyes were always on Agat. No matter who spoke she watched Agat.

"He received me as an equal."

Alla Pasfal nodded approvingly and said, "He always had more sense than the rest of their males." But Seiko went on, "What about the others? Could you just walk through their camp?" Seiko could always dig up his humiliation no matter how well he had buried and forgotten it. His cousin ten times over, his sister-playmate-lover-companion, she possessed an immediate understanding of any weakness in him and any pain he felt, and her sympathy, her compassion closed in on him like a trap. They were too close. Too close, Huru, old Alla, Seiko, all of them. The isolation that had unnerved him today had also given him a glimpse of distance, of solitude, had perhaps waked a craving in him. Seiko gazed at him, watching him with clear, soft, dark eyes, sensitive to his every mood and word. The hilf girl, Rolery, had never yet looked at him, never met his gaze. Her look always was aside, away, glancing, golden, alien.

"They didn't stop me," he answered Seiko briefly. "Well, tomorrow maybe they'll decide on our suggestion. Or the next day. How's the provisioning of the Stack been going this afternoon?" The talk became general, though it tended always to center around and be referred back to Jakob Agat. He was younger than several of them, and all ten Alterrans were elected equal in their ten-year terms on the council, but he was evidently and acknowledgedly their leader, their center. No especial reason for this was visible unless it was the vigor with which he moved and spoke; is authority noticeable in the man, or in the men about him? The effects of it, however, showed in him as a certain tension and somberness, the results of a heavy load of responsibility that he had borne for a long time, and that got daily heavier.

"I made one slip," he said to Pilotson, while Seiko and the other women of the council brewed and served the little, hot, ceremonial cupfuls of steeped basuk leaves called *ti.* "I was trying so hard to convince the old fellow that there really is danger from the Gall, that I think I sent for a moment. Not verbally; but he looked like he'd seen a ghost."

"You've got very powerful sense-projection, and lousy control when you're under strain. He probably did see a ghost."

"We've been out of touch with the hilfs so long—and we're so ingrown here, so damned isolated, I can't trust my control. First I bespeak that girl down on the beach, then I project to Wold—they'll be turning on us as witches if this goes on, the way they did in the first Years. . . . And we've got to get them to trust us. In so short a time. If only we'd known about the Gaal earlier!"

"Well," Pilotson said in his careful way, "since there are

no more human settlements up the coast, it's purely due to your foresight in sending scouts up north that we have any warning at all. Your health, Seiko," he added, accepting the tiny, steaming cup she presented.

Agat took the last cup from her tray, and drained it. There was a slight sense-stimulant in freshly brewed ti, so that he was vividly aware of its astringent, clean heat in his throat, of Seiko's intense gaze, of the bare, large firelit room, of the twilight outside the windows. The cup in his hand, blue porcelain, was very old, a work of the Fifth Year. The handpress books in cases under the windows were old. Even the glass in the windowframes was old. All their luxuries, all that made them civilized, all that kept them Alterran, was old. In Agat's lifetime and for long before there had been no energy or leisure for subtle and complex affirmations of man's skill and spirit. They did well by now merely to preserve, to endure.

Gradually, Year by Year for at least ten generations, their numbers had been dwindling; very gradually, but always there were fewer children born. They retrenched, they drew together. Old dreams of domination were forgotten utterly. They came back—if the Winters and hostile hilf tribes did not take advantage of their weakness first—to the old center, the first colony, Landin. They taught their children the old knowledge and the old ways, but nothing new. They lived always a little more humbly, coming to value the simple over the elaborate, calm over strife, courage over success. They withdrew.

Agat, gazing into the tiny cup in his hand, saw in its clear, pure translucency, the perfect skill of its making and the fragility of its substance, a kind of epitome of the spirit of his people. Outside the high windows the air was the same translucent blue. But cold: a blue twilight, immense and cold. The old terror of his childhood came over Agat, the terror which, as he became adult, he had reasoned thus: this world on which he had been born, on which his father and forefathers for twenty-three generations had been born, was not his home. His kind was alien. Profoundly, they were always aware of it. They were the Farborn. And little by little, with the majestic slowness, the vegetable obstinacy of the process of evolution, this world was killing them—rejecting the graft.

They were perhaps too submissive to this process, too willing to die out. But a kind of submission—their iron adherence to the League Laws—had been their strength from the very beginning; and they were still strong, each one of them. But they had not the knowledge or the skill to combat the sterility and early abortion that reduced their generations. For not all wisdom was written in the League Books, and from day to day and Year to Year a little knowledge would always be lost, supplanted by some more immediately useful bit of information concerning daily existence here and now. And in the end, they could not even understand much of what the books told them. What truly remained of their Heritage, by now? If ever the ship, as in the old hopes and tales, soared down in fire from the stars, would the men who stepped from it know them to be men?

But no ship had come, or would come. They would die; their presence here, their long exile and struggle on this world, would be done with, broken like a bit of clay.

He put the cup very carefully down on the tray, and wiped the sweat off his forehead. Seiko was watching him. He turned from her abruptly and began to listen to Jonkendy, Dermat and Pilotson. Across his bleak rush of foreboding he had recalled briefly, irrelevant and yet seeming both an explanation and a sign, the light, lithe, frightened figure of the girl Rolery, reaching up her hand to him from the dark, sea-besieged stones.

CHAPTER FOUR: *The Tall Young Men*

THE SOUND OF rock pounded on rock, hard and unreverberant, rang out among the roofs and unfinisied walls of the Winter City to the high red tents pitched all around it. *Ak ak ak ak,* the sound went on for a long time, until suddenly a second pounding joined it in count·rpoint, *kadak ak ak kadak.* Another came in on a higher note, giving a tripping rhythm, then another, another, more, until any measure was lost in the clatter of constant sound, an avalanche of the high dry whack of rock hitting rock in which each individual pounding rhythm was submerged, indistinguishable.

As the sound-avalanche went ceaselessly and stupefyingly on, the Eldest Man of the Men of Askatevar walked slowly from his tent and between the aisles of tents and cookfires from which smoke rose through slanting late-afternoon, late-autumn light. Stiff and ponderous the old man went alone through the camp of his people and entered the gate of the Winter City, followed a twisting path or street among the tent-like wooden roofs of the houses, which had no sidewalls aboveground, and came to an open place in the middle of the roofpeaks. There a hundred or so men sat, knees to chin, pounding rock on rock, pounding, in a hypnotic toneless trance of percussion. Wold sat down,

34

completing the circle. He picked up the smaller of two heavy waterworn rocks in front of him and with satisfying heaviness whacked it down on the bigger one: *Klak! klak! klak!* To right and left of him the clatter went on and on, a rattling roar of random noise, through which every now and then a snatch of a certain rhythm could be discerned. The rhythm vanished, recurred, a chance concatenation of noise. On its return Wold caught it, fell in with it and held it. Now to him it dominated the clatter. Now his neighbor to the left was beating it, their two stones rising and falling together; now his neighbor to the right. Now others across the circle were beating it, pounding together. It came clear of the noise, conquered it, forced each conflicting voice into its own single ceaseless rhythm, the concord, the hard heartbeat of the Men of Askatevar, pounding on, and on, and on.

This was all their music, all their dance.

A man leaped up at last and walked into the center of the ring. He was bare-chested, black stripes painted up his arms and legs, his hair a black cloud around his face. The rhythm lightened, lessened, died away. Silence.

"The runner from the north brought news that the Gaal follow the Coast Trail and come in great force. They have come to Tlokna. Have you all heard this?"

A rumble of assent.

"Now listen to the man who called this Stone-Pounding," the shaman-herald called out; and Wold got up with difficulty. He stood in his place, gazing straight ahead, massive, scarred, immobile, an old boulder of a man.

"A farborn came to my tent," he said at last in his age-weakened, deep voice. "He is chief of them in Landin. He said the farborns have grown few and ask the help of men.

A rumble from all the heads of clans and families that sat moveless, knees to chin, in the circle. Over the circle, over the wooden roofpeaks about them, very high up in the cold, golden light, a white bird wheeled, harbinger of winter.

"This farborn said the Southing comes not by clans and

35

tribes but all in one horde, many thousands led by a great chief."

"How does he know?" somebody roared. Protocol was not strict in the Stone-Poundings of Tevar; Tevar had never been ruled by its shamans as some tribes were. "He had scouts up north!" Wold roared back. "He said the Gaal besiege Winter Cities and capture them. That is what the runner said of Tlokna. The farborn says that the warriors of Tevar should join with the farborns and with the men of Pernmek and Allakskat, go up in the north of our range, and turn the Southing aside to the Mountain Trail. These things he said and I heard them. Have you all heard?"

The assent was uneven and turbulent, and a clan chief was on his feet at once. "Eldest! from your mouth we hear the truth always. But when did a farborn speak truth? When did men listen to farborns? I hear nothing this farborn said. What if his City perishes in the Southing? No men live in it! Let them perish and then we men can take their Range."

The speaker, Walmek, was a big dark man full of words; Wold had never liked him, and dislike influenced his reply. "I have heard Walmek. Not for the first time. Are the farborns men or not—who knows? Maybe they fell out of the sky as in the tale. Maybe not. No one ever fell out of the sky this Year . . . They look like men; they fight like men. Their women are like women, I can tell you that! They have some wisdom. It's better to listen to them . . ." His references to farborn women had them all grinning as they sat in their solemn circle, but he wished he had not said it. It was stupid to remind them of his old ties with the aliens. And it was wrong . . . she had been his wife, after all . . .

He sat down, confused, signifying he would speak no more.

Some of the other men, however, were impressed enough by the runner's tale and Agat's warning to argue with those who discounted or distrusted the news. One of Wold's Springborn sons, Umaksuman who loved raids and forays, spoke right out in favor of Agat's plan of marching up to the border.

"It's a trick to get our men away up north on the Range, caught in the first snow, while the farborns steal our flocks and wives and rob the granaries here. They're not men, there's no good in them!" Walmek ranted. Rarely had he found so good a subject to rant on.

"That's all they've ever wanted, our women. No wonder they're growing few and dying out, all they bear is monsters. They want our women so they can bring up human children as theirs!" This was a youngish family-head, very excited. "Aagh!" Wold growled, disgusted at this mishmash of misinformation, but he kept sitting and let Umaksuman set the fellow straight.

"And what if the farborn spoke truth?" Umaksuman went on. "What if the Gaal come through our Range all together, thousands of them? Are we ready to fight them?"

"But the walls aren't finished, the gates aren't up, the last harvest isn't stored," an older man said. This, more than distrust of the aliens, was the core of the question. If the able men marched off to the north, could the women and children and old men finish all the work of readying the Winter City before winter was upon them? Maybe, maybe not. It was a heavy chance to take on the word of a farborn.

Wold himself had made no decision, and looked to abide by that of the Elders. He liked the farborn Agat, and would guess him neither deluded nor a liar; but there was no telling. All men were alien one to another, at times, not only aliens. You could not tell. Perhaps the Gaal were coming as an army. Certainly the Winter was coming. Which enemy first?

The Elders swayed toward doing nothing, but Umaksuman's faction prevailed to the extent of having runners sent to the two neighboring Ranges, Allakskat and Pernmek, to sound them out on the project of a joint defense. That was all the decision made; the shaman released the scrawny hann he had caught in case a decision for war was reached and must be sealed by lapidation, and the Elders dispersed.

Wold was sitting in his tent with men of his Kin over a good hot pot of bhan, when there was a commotion outside. Umaksuman went out, shouted at everybody to clear out, and reentered the great tent behind the farborn Agat.

"Welcome, Alterra," said the old man, and with a sly glance at his two grandsons, "will you sit with us and eat?"

He liked to shock people; he always had. That was why he had always been running off to the farborns in the old days. And this gesture freed him in his mind, from the vague shame he suffered since speaking before the other men of the farborn girl who had so long ago been his wife.

Agat, calm and grave as before, accepted and ate enough to show he took the hospitality seriously; he waited till they were all done eating, and Ukwet's wife had scuttled out with the leavings, then he said, "Eldest, I listen."

"There's not much to hear," Wold replied. He belched. "Runners go to Pernmek and Allakskat. But few spoke for war. The cold grows each day now: safety lies inside walls, under roofs. We don't walk about in timepast as your people do, but we know what the Way of Man has always been and is, and hold to it."

"Your way is good," the farborn said, "good enough, maybe, that the Gaal have learned it from you. In past Winters you were stronger than the Gaal because your clans were gathered together against them. Now the Gaal too have learned that strength lies in numbers."

"*If* that news is true," said Ukwet, who was one of Wold's grandsons, though older than Wold's son Umaksuman.

Agat looked up at him in silence. Ukwet turned aside at once from that straight, dark gaze.

"If it's not true, then why are the Gaal so late coming south?" said Umaksuman. "What's keeping them? Have they ever waited till the harvests were in before?"

"Who knows?" said Wold. "Last Year they came long before the Snowstar rose, I remember that. But who remembers the Year before last?"

"Maybe they're following the Mountain Trail," said the other grandson, "and won't come through Askatevar at all."

"The runner said they had taken Tlokna," Umaksuman said sharply, "and Tlokna is north of Tevar on the Coast Trail. *Why* do we disbelieve this news, why do we wait to act?"

"Because men who fight wars in Winter don't live till Spring," Wold growled.

"But if they come—"

"If they come, we'll fight."

There was a little pause. Agat for once looked at none of them, but kept his dark gaze lowered like a human.

"People say," Ukwet remarked with a jeering note, sensing triumph, "that the farborns have strange powers. I know nothing about all that, I was born on the Summerlands and never saw farborns before this moonphase, let alone sat to eat with one. But if they're witches and have such powers, why would they need our help against the Gaal?"

"I do not hear you!" Wold thundered, his face purple and his eyes watering. Ukwet hit his face. Enraged by this insolence to a tent-guest, and by his own confusion and indecisiveness which made him argue against both sides, Wold sat breathing heavily, staring with inflamed eyes at the young man, who kept his face hidden.

"I talk," Wold said at last, his voice still loud and deep, free for a little from the huskiness of old age. "I talk: listen! Runners will go up the Coast Trail until they meet the Southing. And behind them, two days behind, but no farther than the border of our Range, warriors will follow—all men born between Midspring and the Summer Fallow. If the Gaal come in force, the warriors will drive them east to the mountains; if not, they will come back to Tevar."

Umaksuman laughed aloud and said, "Eldest, no man leads us but you!"

Wold growled and belched and settled down. "You'll lead the warriors, though," he told Umaksuman dourly.

Agat, who had not spoken for some time, said in his quiet way, "My people can send three hundred and fifty men. We'll go up the old beach road, and join with your men at the border of Askatevar." He rose and held out his hand. Sulky at having been driven into this commitment, and still shaken by his emotion, Wold ignored him. Umaksuman was on his feet in a flash, his hand against the farborn's. They stood there for a moment in the firelight like day and night. Agat dark, shadowy, somber, Umaksuman fair-skinned, light-eyed, radiant.

The decision was made, and Wold knew he could force it upon the other Elders. He knew also that it was the last decision he would ever make. He could send them to war: but Umaksuman would come back, the leader of the war-riors, and thereby the strongest leader among the Men of Askatevar. Wold's action was his own abdication. Umaksuman would be the young chief. He would close the circle of the Stone-Pounding, he would lead the hunters in Winter, the forays in Spring, the great wanderings of the long days of Summer. His Year was just beginning . . .

"Go on," Wold growled at them all. "Call the Stone-Pounding for tomorrow, Umaksuman. Tell the shaman to stake out a hann, a fat one with some blood in it." He would not speak to Agat. They left, all the tall young men. He sat crouched on his stiff hams by his fire, staring into the yellow flames as if into the heart of a lost brightness, Summer's irrecoverable warmth.

CHAPTER FIVE: *Twilight in the Woods*

THE FARBORN CAME out of Umaksuman's tent and stood
a minute talking with the young chief, both of them looking
to the north, eyes narrowed against the biting gray wind.
Agat moved his outstretched hand as if he spoke of the
mountains. A flaw of wind carried a word or two of what he
said to Rolery where she stood watching on the path up to
the city gate. As she heard him speak a tremor went through
her, a little rush of fear, and darkness through her veins,
making her remember how that voice had spoken in her
mind, in her flesh, calling her to him.

Behind that like a distorted echo in her memory came
the harsh command, outward as a slap, when on the forest
path he had turned on her, telling her to go, to get away
from him.

All of a sudden she put down the baskets she was carrying. They were moving today from the red tents of her nomad childhood into the warren of peaked roofs and underground halls and tunnels and alleys of the Winter City, and
all her cousin-sisters and aunts and nieces were bustling
and squealing and scurrying up and down the paths and in
and out of the tents and the gates with furs and boxes and
branches tearing at her clothes, catching her hood. The
there beside the path and walked off toward the forest.

"Rolery! Ro-o-olery!" shrilled the voices that were forever shrilling after her, accusing, calling, screeching at her back. She never turned, but walked right on. As soon as she was well into the woods she began to run. When all sound of voices was lost in the soughing, groaning silence of the wind-strained trees, and nothing recalled the camp of her people except a faint, bitter scent of woodsmoke in the wind, she slowed down.

Great fallen trunks barred the path now in places, and must be climbed over or crawled under, the stiff dead branches tearing at her clothes, cathcing her hood. The woods were not safe in this wind; even now, somewhere off up the ridge she heard the muttering crash of a tree falling before the wind's push. She did not care. She felt like going down onto those gray sands again and standing still, perfectly still, to watch the foaming thirty-foot wall of water come down upon her . . . As suddenly as she had started off, she stopped, and stood still on the twilit path.

The wind blew and ceased and blew. A murky sky writhed and lowered over the network of leafless branches. It was already half dark here. All anger and purpose drained out of the girl, leaving her standing in a kind of scared stupor, hunching her shoulders against the wind. Something white flashed in front of her and she cried out, but did not move. Again the white movement passed, then stilled suddenly above her on a jagged branch: a great beast or bird, winged, pure white, white above and below, with short, sharp hooked lips that parted and closed, and staring silver eyes. Gripping the branch with four naked talons the creature gazed down at her, and she up at it, neither moving. The silver eyes never blinked. Abruptly great white wings shot out, wider than a man's height, and beat among the branches, breaking them. The creature beat its white wings and screamed, then as the wind gusted launched out into the air and made its way heavily off between the branches and the driving clouds.

"A stormbringer." Agat spoke, standing on the path a

few yards behind her. "They're supposed to bring the blizzards."

The great silver creature had driven all her wits away. The little rush of tears that accompanied all strong feelings in her race blinded her a moment. She had meant to stand and mock him, to jeer at him, having seen the resentment under his easy arrogance when people in Tevar slighted him, treated him as what he was, a being of a lower kind. But the white creature, the stormbringer, had frightened her and she broke out, staring straight at him as she had at it, "I hate you, you're not a man, I hate you!"

Then her tears stopped, she looked away, and they both stood there in silence for quite a while.

"Rolery," said the quiet voice, "look at me."

She did not. He came forward, and she drew back crying, "Don't touch me!" in a voice like the stormbringer's scream, her face distorted. "Get hold of yourself," he said. "Here—take my hand, take it!" He caught her as she struggled to break away, and held both her wrists. Again they stood without moving.

"Let me go," she said at last in her normal voice. He released her at once.

She drew a long breath.

"You spoke—I heard you speak inside me. Down there on the sands. Can you do that again?"

He was watching her, alert and quiet. He nodded. "Yes. But I told you then that I never would."

"I still hear it. I feel your voice." She put her hands over her ears.

"I know . . . I'm sorry. I didn't know you were a hilf— a Tevaran, when I called you. It's against the law. And anyhow it shouldn't have worked . . ."

"What's a hilf?"

"What we call you."

"What do you call yourselves?"

"Men."

She looked around them at the groaning twilit woods, gray aisles, writhing cloud-roof. This gray world in motion was very strange, but she was no longer scared. His touch, his actual hand's touch canceling the insistent impalpable sense of his presence, had given her calm, which grew as they spoke together. She saw now that she had been half out of her mind this last day and night.

"Can all your people do that . . . speak that way?"

"Some can. It's a skill one can learn. Takes practice. Come here, sit down a while. You've had it rough." He was always harsh and yet there was an edge, a hint of something quite different in his voice now: as if the urgency with which he had called to her on the sands were transmuted into an infinitely restrained, unconscious appeal, a reaching out. They sat down on a fallen basuk-tree a couple of yards off the path. She noticed how differently he moved and sat than a man of her race; the schooling of his body, the sum of his gestures, was very slightly, but completely, unfamiliar. She was particularly aware of his dark-skinned hands, clasped together between his knees. He went on, "Your people could learn mindspeech if they wanted to. But they never have, they call it witchcraft, I think . . . Our books say that we ourselves learned it from another race, long ago, on a world called Rokanan. It's a skill as well as a gift."

"Can you *hear* my mind when you want?"

"That is forbidden," he said with such finality that her fears on that score were quite disposed of.

"Teach me the skill," she said with sudden childishness.

"It would take all Winter."

"It took you all fall?"

"And part of Summer too." He grinned slightly.

"What does hilf mean?"

"It's a word from our old language. It means 'Highly intelligent life-form.' "

"Where is another world?"

"Well—there are a lot of them. Out there. Beyond sun and moon."

"Then you did fall out of the sky? What for? How did you get from behind the sun to the seacoast here?"

"I'll tell you if you want to hear, but it's not just a tale, Rolery. There's a lot we don't understand, but what we do know of our history is true."

"I hear," she whispered in the ritual phrase, impressed, but not entirely subdued.

"Well, there were many worlds out among the stars, and many kinds of men living on them. They made ships that could sail the darkness between the worlds, and kept traveling about and trading and exploring. They allied themselves into a League, as your clans ally with one another to make a Range. But there was an enemy of the League of All Worlds. An enemy coming from far off. I don't know how far. The books were written for men who knew more than we know . . ."

He was always using words that sounded like words, but meant nothing; Rolery wondered what a ship was, what a book was. But the grave, yearning tone in which he told his story worked on her and she listened fascinated.

"For a long time the League prepared to fight that enemy. The stronger worlds helped the weaker ones to arm against the enemy, to make ready. A little as we're trying to make ready to meet the Gaal, here. Mindhearing was one skill they taught, I know, and there were weapons, the books say fires that could burn up whole planets and burst the stars . . . Well, during that time my people came from their home-world to this one. Not very many of them. They were to make friends with your peoples and see if they wanted to be a world of the League, and join against the enemy. But the enemy came. The ship that brought my people went back to where it came from, the help in fighting the war, and some of the people went with it, and the . . . the far-speaker with which those men could talk to one another from world to world. But some of the people

45

stayed on here, either to help this world if the enemy came here, or because they couldn't go back again: we don't know. Their records say only that the ship left. A white spear of metal, longer than a whole city, standing up on a feather of fire. There are pictures of it. I think they thought it would come back soon . . . That was ten Years ago."

"What of the war with the enemy?"

"We don't know. We don't know anything that happened since the day the ship left. Some of us figure the war must have been lost, and others think it was won, but hardly, and the few men left here were forgotten in the years of fighting. Who knows? If we survive, some day we'll find out; if no one ever comes, we'll make a ship and go find out . . ." He was yearning, ironic. Rolery's head spun with these gulfs of time and space and incomprehension. "This is hard to live with," she said after a while.

Agat laughed, as if startled. "No—it gives us our pride. What is hard is to keep alive on a world you don't belong to. Five Years ago we were a great people. Look at us now."

"They say farborns are never sick, is that true?"

"Yes. We don't catch your sicknesses, and didn't bring any of our own. But we bleed when we're cut, you know . . . And we get old, we die, like humans . . ."

"Well of course," she said disgustedly.

He dropped his sarcasm. "Our trouble is that we don't bear enough children. So many abort and are stillborn, so few come to term."

"I heard that. I thought about it. You do so strangely. You conceive children any time of the Year, during the Winter Fallow even—why is that?"

"We can't help it, it's how we are." He laughed again, looking at her, but she was very serious now. "I was born out of season, in the Summer Fallow," she said. "It does happen with us, but very rarely; and you see—when Winter's over I'll be too old to bear a Spring child. I'll never have a son. Some old man will take me for a fifth wife one of these days, but the Winter Fallow has begun, and come

46

Spring I'll be old . . . So I will die barren. It's better for a woman not to be born at all than to be born out of season as I was . . . And another thing, it is true what they say, that a farborn man takes only one wife?"

He nodded. Apparently that meant what a shrug meant to her.

"Well, no wonder you're dying out!"

He grinned, but she insisted, "Many wives—many sons. If you were a Tevaran you'd have five or ten children already! Have you any?"

"No, I'm not married."

"But haven't you ever lain with a woman!"

"Well, yes," he said, and then more assertively, "Of course! But when we want children, we marry."

"If you were one of us—"

"But I'm not one of you," he said. Silence ensued. Finally he said, gently enough, "It isn't manners and mores that make the difference. We don't know what's wrong, but it's in the seed. Some doctors have thought that because this sun's different from the sun our race was born under, it affects us, changes the seed in us little by little. And the change kills."

Again there was silence between them for a time. "What was the other world like—your home?"

"There are songs that tell what it was like," he said, but when she asked timidly what a song was, he did not reply. After a while he said, "At home, the world was closer to its sun, and the whole year there wasn't even one moonphase long. So the books say. Think of it, the whole Winter would only last ninety days . . ." This made them both laugh. "You wouldn't have time to light a fire," Rolery said.

Real darkness was soaking into the dimness of the woods. The path in front of them ran indistinct, a faint gap among the trees leading left to her city, right to his. Here, between, was only wind, dusk, solitude. Night was coming quickly. Night and winter and war, a time of dying. "I'm afraid of the Winter," she said, very low.

"We all are," he said. "What will it be like? . . . We've only known the sunlight."

There was no one among her people who had ever broken her fearless, careless solitude of mind; having no age-mates, and by choice also, she had always been quite alone, going her own way and caring little for any person. But now as the world had turned gray and nothing held any promise beyond death, now as she first felt fear, she had met him, the dark figure near the tower-rock over the sea, and had heard a voice that spoke in her blood.

"Why will you never look at me?" he asked.

"I will," she said, "if you want me to." But she did not, though she knew his strange shadowy gaze was on her. At last she put out her hand and he took it.

"Your eyes are gold," he said. "I want . . . I want . . . But if they knew we were together, even now . . ."

"Your people?"

"Yours. Mine care nothing about it."

"And mine needn't find out." They both spoke almost in whispers, but urgently, without pauses.

"Rolery, I leave for the north two nights from now."

"I know that."

"When I come back—"

"But when you don't come back!" the girl cried out, under the pressure of the terror that had entered her with Autumn's end, the fear of coldness, of death. He held her against him telling her quietly that he would come back. As he spoke she felt the beating of his heart and the beating of her own. "I want to stay with you," she said, and he was saying, "I want to stay with you."

It was dark around them. When they got up they walked slowly in a grayish darkness. She came with him, towards his city. "Where can we go?" he said with a kind of bitter laugh. "This isn't like love in Summer . . . There's a hunter's shelter down the ridge a way . . . They'll miss you in Tevar."

"No," she whispered, "they won't miss me."

CHAPTER SIX: *Snow*

THE FORE-RUNNERS had gone; tomorrow the Men of
Askatevar would march north on the broad vague trail that
divided their Range, while the smaller group from Landin
would take the old road up the coast. Like Agat, Umaksuman had judged it best to keep the two forces apart until the
eve of fighting. They were allied only by Wold's authority.
Many of Umaksuman's men, though veterans of many
raids and forays before the Winter Peace, were reluctant to
go on this unseasonal war; and a sizable faction, even within his own Kin, so detested this alliance with the farborns
that they were ready to make any trouble they could. Ukwet and others had said openly that when they had finished
with the Gaal they would finish off the witches. Agat discounted this, foreseeing that victory would modify, and de-
feat end, their prejudice; but it worried Umaksuman, who
did not look so far ahead.

"Our scouts will keep you in sight all along. After all, the
Gaal may not wait on the border for us."

"The Long Valley under Cragtop would be a good place
for a battle," Umaksuman said with his flashing smile.
"Good luck, Alterra!"

"Good luck to you, Umaksuman." They parted as
friends, there under the mud-cemented stone gateway of
the Winter City. As Agat turned something flickered in the

dull afternoon air beyond the arch, a wavering drifting movement. He looked up startled, then turned back. "Look at that."

The native came out from the walls and stood beside him a minute, to see for the first time the stuff of old men's tales. Agat held his hand out palm up. A flickering speck of white touched his wrist and was gone. The long vale of stubble-fields and used-up pasture, the creek, the dark inlet of the forest and the farther hills to south and west all seemed to tremble very slightly, to withdraw, as random flakes fell from the low sky, twirling and slanting a little, though the wind was down.

Children's voices cried in excitement behind them among the high-peaked wooden roofs.

"Snow is smaller than I thought," Umaksuman said at last, dreamily.

"I thought it would be colder. The air seems warmer than it did before . . ." Agat roused himself from the sinsiter and charming fascination of the twirling fall of the snow. "Til we meet in the north," he said, and pulling his fur collar close around his neck against the queer, searching touch of the tiny flakes, set out on the path to Landin.

A half-kilo into the forest he saw the scarcely marked side path that led to the hunter's shelter, and passing it felt as if his veins were running liquid light. "Come on, come on," he told himself, impatient with his recurrent loss of self-control. He had got the whole thing perfectly straight in the short intervals for thinking he had had today. Last night—had been last night. All right, it was that and nothing more. Aside from the fact that she was, after all, a hilf and he was human, so there was no future in the thing, it was foolish on other counts. Ever since he had seen her face, on the black steps over the tide, he had thought of her and yearned to see her, like an adolescent mooning after his first girl; and if there was anything he hated it was the stupidity, the obstinate stupidity of uncontrolled passion. It led men to take blind risks, to hazard really important things for a mere moment of lust, to lose control over their acts. So, in order to stay in control, he had gone with her last night; that was merely sensible to get the fit over with. So he told himself once more, walking along very rapidly, his head high, while the snow danced thinly around him. To-night he would meet her again, for the same reason. At the thought, a flood of warm light and an aching joy ran through his body and mind; he ignored it. Tomorrow he was off to the north, and if he came back, then there would be time enough to explain to the girl that there could be no more such nights, no more lying together on his fur cloak in the shelter in the forest's heart, starlight overhead and the cold and the great silence all around . . . no, no more . . . The absolute happiness she had given him came up in him like a tide, drowning all thought. He ceased to tell himself anything. He walked rapidly with his long stride in the gathering darkness of the woods, and as he walked, sang under his breath, not knowing that he did so, some old love-song of his exiled race.

The snow scarcely penetrated the branches. It was getting dark very early, he thought as he approached the place where the path divided, and this was the last thing in his mind when something caught his ankle in midstride and sent him pitching forward. He landed on his hands and was half-way up when a shadow on his left became a man, silvery-white in the gloom, who knocked him over before he was fairly up. Confused by the ringing in his ears, Agat struggled free of something holding him and again tried to stand up. He seemed to have lost his bearings and did not understand what was happening, though he had an impression that it had happened before, and also that it was not actually happening. There were several more of the silvery-looking men with stripes down their legs and arms, and they held him by the arms while another one came up and struck him with something across the mouth. There was pain, the darkness was full of pain and rage. With a furious and skillful convulsion of his whole body he got free of the silvery men, catching one under the jaw with his fist and sending him out of the scene backward: but there were more and more of them and he could not get free a second time. They hit him and when he hid his face in his arms against the mud of the path they kicked his sides. He lay pressed against the blessed harmless mud, trying to hide, and heard somebody breathing very strangely. Through that noise he also heard Umaksuman's voice. Even he, then . . . But he did not care, so long as they would go away, would let him be. It was getting dark very early.

It was dark: pitch dark. He tried to crawl forward. He wanted to get home to his people who would help him. It was so dark he could not see his hands. Soundlessly and unseen in the absolute blackness, snow fell on him and around him on the mud and leafmold. He wanted to get home. He was very cold. He tried to get up, but there was no west or east, and sick with pain he put his head down on his arm. "Come to me," he tried to call in the mindspeech of Alterra, but it was to hard to call so far into the darkness. It was easier to lie still right here. Nothing could be easier.

In a high stone house in Landin, by a driftwood fire, Alla Pasfal lifted her head suddenly from her book. She had a distinct impression that Jakob Agat was sending to her, but no message came. It was queer. There were all too many queer by-products and aftereffects and inexplicables involved in mindspeech; many people here in Landin never learned it, and those who did used it very sparingly. Up north in Atlantika colony they had mindspoken more freely. She herself was a refugee from Atlantika and remembred how in the terrible Winter of her childhood she had mindspoken with the others all the time. And after her mother and father died in the famine, for a whole moonphase after, over and over again she had felt them sending to her, felt their presence in her mind—but no message, no words, silence.

"Jakob!" She bespoke him, long and hard, but there was no answer.

52

At the same time, in the Armory checking over the expedition's supplies once more, Huru Pilotson abruptly gave way to the uneasiness that had been preying on him all day and burst out, "What the hell does Agat think he's doing!"

"He's pretty late," one of the Armory boys affirmed. "Is he over at Tevar again?"

"Cementing relations with the mealy-faces," Pilotson said, gave a mirthless giggle, and scowled. "All right, come on, let's see about the parkas."

At the same time, in a room paneled with wood like ivory satin, Seiko Esmit burst into a fit of silent crying, wringing her hands and struggling not to send to him, not to bespeak him, not even to whisper his name aloud:"Jakob!"

At the same time Rolery's mind went quite dark for a while. She simply crouched motionless where she was.

She was in the hunter's shelter. She had thought, with all the confusion of the move from the tents into the warren-like Kinhouses of the city, that her absence and very late return had not been observed last night. But today was different; order was reestablished and her leaving would be seen. So she had gone off in broad daylight as she so often did, trusting that no one would take special notice of that; she had gone circuitously to the shelter, curled down there in her furs and waited till dark should fall and finally he should come. The snow had begun to fall; watching it made her sleepy; she watched it, wondering sleepily what she would do tomorrow. For he would be gone. And everyone in her clan would know she had been out all night. That was tomorrow. It would take care of itself. This was tonight, tonight . . . and she dozed off, till suddenly she woke with a great start, and crouched there a little while, her mind blank, dark.

Then abruptly she scrambled up and with flint and tinderbox lighted the basket-lantern she had brought with her. By its tiny glow she headed downhill till she struck the path, then hesitated, and turned west. Once she stopped and said,

"Alterra . . ." in a whisper. The forest was perfectly quiet in the night. She went on till she found him lying across the path.

The snow, falling thicker now, streaked across the lantern's dim, small glow. The snow was sticking to the ground now instead of melting, and it had stuck in a powdering of white all over his torn coat and even on his hair. His hand, which she touched first, was cold and she knew he was dead. She sat down on the wet, snow-rimmed mud by him and took his head on her knees.

He moved and made a kind of whimper, and with that Rolery came to herself. She stopped her silly gesture of smoothing the powdery snow from his hair and collar, and sat intent for a minute. Then she eased him back down, got up, automatically tried to rub the sticky blood from her hand, and with the lantern's aid began to seek around the sides of the path for something. She found what she needed and set to work.

Soft, weak sunlight slanted down across the room. In that warmth it was hard to wake up and he kept sliding back down into the waters of sleep, the deep tideless lake. But the light always brought him up again; and finally he was awake, seeing the high gray walls about him and the slant of sunlight through glass.

He lay still while the shaft of watery golden light faded and returned, slipped from the floor and pooled on the farther wall, rising higher, reddening. Alla Pasfal came in, and seeing he was awake signed to someone behind her to stay out. She closed the door and came to kneel by him. Alterran houses were sparsely furnished; they slept on pallets on the carpeted floor, and for chairs used at most a thin cushion. So Alla knelt, and looked down at Agat, her worn, black face lighted strongly by the reddish shaft of sun. There was no pity in her face as she looked at him. She had borne too much, too young, for compassion and scruple ever to rise from very deep in her, and in her old age she was quite pitiless. She shok her head a little from side to side as she said softly, "Jakob . . . What have you done?"

He found that his head hurt him when he tried to speak, so having no real answer he kept still.

"What have you done . . ."

"How did I get home?" he asked at last, forming the words so poorly with his smashed mouth that she raised her hand to stop him. "How you got here—is that what you asked? She brought you. The hilf girl. She made a sort of travois out of some branches and her furs, and rolled you onto it and hauled you over the ridge and to the Land Gate. At night in the snow. Nothing left on her but her breeches —she had to tear up her tunic to tie you on. Those hilfs are tougher than the leather they dress in. She said the snow made it easier to pull . . . No snow left now. That was night before last. You've had a pretty good rest all in all."

She poured him a cup of water from the jug on a tray nearby and helped him drink. Close over him her face looked very old, delicate with age. She said to him with the mindspeech, unbelievingly, *How could you do this? You were always a proud man, Jakob!*

He replied the same way, wordlessly. Put into words what he told her was: *I can't get on without her.*

The old woman flinched physically away from the sense of his passion, and as if in self-defense spoke aloud: "But what a time to pick for a love affair, for a romance! When everyone depended on you—"

He repeated what he had told her, for it was the truth and all he could tell her. She bespoke him with harshness: *But you're not going to marry her, so you'd better learn to get on without her.*

He replied only, *No.*

She sat back on her heels a while. When her mind opened again to his it was with a great depth of bitterness. *Well, go ahead, what's the difference. At this point whatever we do, any of us, alone or together, is wrong. We can't do the right thing, the lucky thing. We can only go on committing sui-*

cide, little by little, one by one. Till we're all gone, till Al-terra is gone, all the exiles dead . . .

"Alla," he broke in aloud, shaken by her despair, "the . . . the men went . . . ?"

"What men? Our army?" She said the words sarcastical-ly. "Did they march north yesterday—without you?"

"Pilotson—"

"If Pilotson had led them anywhere it would have been to attack Tevar. To avenge you. He was crazy with rage yesterday."

"And they . . ."

"The hilfs? No, of course they didn't go. When it became known that Wold's daughter is running off to sleep with a farborn in the woods, Wold's faction comes in for a certain amount of ridicule and discredit—you can see that? Of course, it's easier to see it after the fact; but I should have thought—"

"For God's sake, Alla."

"All right. Nobody went north. We sit here and wait for the Gaal to arrive when they please."

Jakob Agat lay very still, trying to keep himself from falling headfirst, backwards, into the void that lay under him. It was the blank and real abyss of his own pride: the self-deceiving arrogance from which all his acts had sprung: the lie. If he went under, no matter. But what of his people whom he had betrayed?

Alla bespoke him after a while: *Jakob, it was a very little hope at best. You did what you could. Man and unman can't work together. Six hundred home-years of failure should tell you that. Your folly was only their pretext. If they hadn't turned on us over it, they would have found something else very soon. They're our enemies as much as the Gaal. Or the Winter. Or the rest of this planet that doesn't want us. We can make no alliances but among our-selves. We're on our own. Never hold your hand out to any creature that belongs to this world.*

He turned his mind away from hers, unable to endure the

56

finality of her despair. He tried to lie closed in on himself, withdrawn, but something worried him insistently, dragged at his consciousness, until suddenly it came clear, and struggling to sit up he stammered, "Where is she? You didn't send her back—"

Clothed in a white Alterran robe, Rolery sat crosslegged, a little farther away from him than Alla had been. Alla was gone; Rolery sat there busy with some work, mending a sandal it seemed. She had not seemed to notice that he spoke; perhaps he had only spoken in dream. But she said presently in her light voice, "That old one upset you. She could have waited. What can you do now? . . . I think none of them knows how to take six steps without you."

The last red of the sunlight made a dull glory on the wall behind her. She sat with a quiet face, eyes cast down as always, absorbed in mending a sandal.

In her presence both guilt and pain eased off and took their due proportion. With her, he was himself. He spoke her name aloud.

"Oh, sleep now; it hurts you to talk," she said with a flicker of her timid mockery.

"Will you stay?" he asked.

"Yes."

"As my wife," he insisted, reduced by necessity and pain to the bare essential. He imagined that her people would kill her if she went back to them; he was not sure what his own people might do to her. He was her only defense, and he wanted the defense to be certain.

She bowed her head as if in acceptance; he did not know her gestures well enough to be sure. He wondered a little at her quietness now. The little while he had known her she had always been quick with motion and emotion. But it had been a very little while . . . As she sat there working away her quietness entered into him, and with it he felt his strength begin to return.

CHAPTER SEVEN: *The Southing*

BRIGHT ABOVE the roofpeaks burned the star whose rising told the start of Winter, as cheerlessly birght as Wold remembered it from his boyhood sixty moonphases ago. Even the great, slender crescent moon opposite it in the sky seemed paler than the Snowstar. A new moonphase had begun, and a new season. But not auspiciously.

Was it ture what the farborns used to say, that the moon was a world like Askatevar and the other Ranges, though without living creatures, and the stars too were worlds, where men and beasts lived and summer and winter came? . . . What sort of men would dwell on the Snowstar? Terrible beings, white as snow, with pallid lipless mouths and fiery eyes, stalked through Wold's imagaination. He shook his head and tried to pay attention to what the other Elders were saying. The fore-runners had returned after only five days with various rumors from the north; and the Elders had built a fire in the great court of Tevar and held a Stone-Pounding. Wold had come last and closed the circle, for no other man dared; but it was meaningless, humiliating to him. For the war he had declared was not being fought, the men he had sent had not gone, and the alliance he had made was broken.

Beside him, as silent as he, sat Umaksuman. The others shouted and wrangled, getting nowhere. What did they expect? No rhythm had risen out of the pounding of stones, there had been only clatter and conflict. After that, could they expect to agree on anything? Fools, fools, Wold thought, glowering at the fire that was too far away to warm him. The others were mostly younger, they could keep warm with youth and with shouting at one another. But he was an old man and furs did not warm him, out under the glaring Snowstar in the wind of Winter. His legs ached now with cold, his chest hurt, and he did not know or care what they were all quarreling about.

Umaksuman was suddenly on his feet. "Listen!" he said, and the thunder of his voice (*He got that from me,* thought Wold) compelled them, though there were audible mutters and jeers. So far, though everybody had a fair idea what had happened, the immediate cause or pretext of their quarrel with Landin had not been discussed outside the walls of Wold's Kinhouse; it had simply been announced that Umaksuman was not to lead the foray, that there was to be no foray, that there might be an attack from the far-borns. Those of other houses who knew nothing about Rolery or Agat knew what was actually involved: a power-struggle between factions in the most powerful clan. This was covertly going on in every speech made now in the Stone-Pounding, the subject of which was, nominally, whether the farborns were to be treated as enemies when met beyond the walls.

Now Umaksuman spoke: "Listen, Elders of Tevar! You say this, you say that, but you have nothing left to say. The Gaal are coming: within three days they are here. Be silent and go sharpen your spears, go look to our gates and walls, because the enemy comes, they come down on us—see!" He flung out his arm to the north, and many turned to stare where he pointed, as if expecting the hordes of the Southing to burst through the wall that moment, so urgent was Umaksuman's rhetoric.

"Why didn't you look to the gate your kinswoman went out of, Umaksuman?"

Now it was said.

"She's your kinswoman too, Ukwet," Umaksuman said wrathfully.

One of them was Wold's son, the other his grandson; they spoke of his daughter. For the first time in his life Wold knew shame, bald, helpless shame before all the best men of his people. He sat moveless, his head bowed down.

"Yes, she is; and because of me, no shame rests on our Kin! I and my brothers knocked the teeth out of the dirty face of that one she lay with, and I had him down to geld him as he-animals should be gelded, but then you stopped us, Umaksuman. You stopped us with your fool talk—"

"I stopped you so that we wouldn't have the farborns to fight along with the Gaal, you fool! She's of age to sleep with a man if she chooses, and this is no—"

"He was no man, kinsman, and I am no fool."

"You are a fool, Ukwet, for you jumped at this as a chance to make quarrel with the farborns, and so lost us our one chance to turn aside the Gaal!"

"I do not hear you, liar, traitor!"

They met with a yell in the middle of the circle, axes drawn. Wold got up. Men sitting near him looked up expecting him, as Eldest and clan-chief, to stop the fight. But he did not. He turned away from the broken circle and in silence, with his stiff, ponderous shuffle, went down the alley between the high slant roofs, under projecting eaves, to the house of his Kin.

He clambered laboriously down earthen stairs into the stuffy, smoky warmth of the immense dug-out room. Boys and womenfolk came asking him if the Stone-Pounding was over and why he came alone. "Umaksuman and Ukwet are fighting," he said to get rid of them, and sat down by the fire, his legs right in the firepit. No good would come of this. No good would come of anything any more. When crying women brought in the body of his grandson Ukwet, a thick path of blood dropping behind them from the ax-split skull, he looked on without moving or speaking.

"Umaksuman killed him, his kinsman, his brother," Uk-wet's wives shrilled at Wold, who never raised his head. Finally he looked around at them heavily like an old animal beset by hunters, and said in a thick voice, "Be still . . . Can't you be still . . ."

It snowed again next day. They buried Ukwet, the first-dead of the Winter, and the snow fell on the corpse's face before the grave was filled. Wold thought then and later of Umaksuman, outlawed, alone in the hills, in the snow. Which was better off?

His tongue was very thick and he did not like to talk. He stayed by the fire and was not sure, sometimes, whether outside it was day or night. He did not sleep well; he seemed somehow always to be waking up. He was just waking up when the noise began outside, up above ground.

Women came shrieking in from the side-rooms, grabbing up their little Fall-born brats. "The Gaal, the Gaal!" they screeched. Others were quiet as befitted women of a great house, and put the place in order and sat down to wait.

No man came for Wold.

He knew he was no longer a chief; but was he no longer a man? Must he stay with the babies and women by the fire, in a hole in the ground?

He had endured public shame, but the loss of his own self-respect he could not endure, and shaking a little he got up and began to rummage in his old painted chest for his leather vest and his heavy spear, the spear with which he had killed a snow-ghoul singlehanded, very long ago. He was stiff and heavy now and all the bright seasons had passed since then, but he was the same man, the same that had killed with that spear in the snow of another winter. Was he not the same man? They should not have left him here by the fire, when the enemy came.

His fool womenfolk came squealing around him, and he got mixed up and angry. But old Kerly drove them all off, gave him back his spear that one of them had taken from him, and fastened at his neck the cape of gray korio-fur she had made for him in autumn. There was one left who knew what a man was. She watched him in silence and he felt her grieving pride. So he walked very erect. She was a cross old woman and he was a foolish old man, but pride remained. He climbed up into the cold, bright noon, hearing beyond the walls the calling of foreign voices.

Men were gathered on the square platform over the smokehold of the House of Absence. They made way for him when he hoisted himself up the ladder. He was wheezing and trembling so that at first he could see nothing. Then he saw. For a while he forgot everything in the unbelievable sight.

The valley that wound from north to south along the base of Tevar Hill to the river-valley east of the forest was full—full as the river in the flood-time, swarming, overrunning with people. They were moving southward, a sluggish, jumbled, dark flood, stretching and contracting, stopping and starting, with yells, cries, calls, creaking, snapping whips, the hoarse bray of hann, the wail of babies, the tuneless chanting of travois-pullers; the flash of color from a rolled-up red felt tent, a woman's painted bangles, a red plume, a spearhead; the stink, the noise, the movement—always the movement, moving southward, the Southing. But in all timepast there had never been a Southing like this, so many all together. As far as eye could follow up the widening valley northward there were more coming, and behind them more, and behind them more. And these were only the women and the brats and the baggage-train . . . Beside that slow torrent of people the Winter City of Tevar was nothing. A pebble on the edge of a river in flood.

At first Wold felt sick; then he took heart, and said presently, "This is a wonderful thing . . ." And it was, this migration of all the nations of the north. He was glad to have seen it. The man next to him, an Elder, Anweld of Siokman's Kin, shrugged and answered quietly, "But it's the end of us."

"If they stop here."

"These won't. But the warriors come behind."

They were so strong, so safe in their numbers, that their warriors came behind. . . .

"They'll need our stores and our herds tonight, to feed all those," Anweld went on. "As soon as these get by, they'll attack."

"Send our women and children out into the hills to the west, then. This City is only a trap against such a force."

"I listen," Anweld said with a shrug of assent.

"Now—quickly—before the Gaal encircle us."

"This has been said and heard. But others say we can't send our women out to fend for themselves while we stay in the shelter of the walls."

"Then let's go with them!" Wold growled. "Can the Men of Tevar decide nothing?"

"They have no leader," Anweld said. "They follow this man and that man and no man." To say more would be to seem to blame Wold and his kinsmen; he said no more except, "So we wait here to be destroyed."

"I'm going to send my womenfolk off," Wold said, irked by Anweld's cool hopelessness, and he left the mighty spectacle of the Southing, to lower himself down the ladder and go tell his kinfolk to save themselves while there was some chance. He meant to go with them. For there was no fighting such odds, and some, some few of the people of Tevar must survive.

But the younger men of his clan did not agree and would not take his orders. They would stand and fight.

"But you'll die," said Wold, "and your women and children might go free—if they're not here with you." His tongue was thick again. They could hardly wait for him to finish.

"We'll beat off the Gaal," said a young grandson. "We are warriors!"

"Tevar is a strong city, Eldest," another said, persuasive, flattering. "You told us and taught us to build it well."

"It will stand against Winter," Wold said. "Not against ten thousand warriors. I would rather see my women die of the cold in the bare hills, than live as whores and slaves of the Gaal." But they were not listening, only waiting for him to be done talking.

He went outside again, but was too weary now to climb the ladders to the platform again. He found himself a place to wait out of the way of the coming and going in the narrow alleys: a niche by a supporting buttress of the south wall, not far from the gate. If he clambered up on the slanting mud-brick buttress he could look over the wall and watch the Southing going by; when the wind got under his cape he could squat down, chin on knees, and have some shelter in the angle. For a while the sun shone on him there. He squatted in its warmth and did not think of much. Once or twice he glanced up at the sun, the Winter sun, old, weak in its old age.

Winter grasses, the short-lived hasty-flowering little plants that would thrive between the blizzards until midwinter when the snow did not melt and nothing lived but the rootless snowcrop, already were pushing up through the trampled ground under the wall. Always something lived, each creature biding its time through the great Year, flourishing and dying down to wait again.

The long hours went by.

There was crying and shouting at the northwest corner of the walls. Men went running by through the ways of the little city, alleys wide enough for one man only under the overhanging eaves. Then the roar of shouting was behind Wold's back and outside the gate to his left. The high wooden slidegate, that lifted from inside by means of long pulleys, rattled in its frame. They were ramming a log against it. Wold got up with difficulty; he had got so stiff sitting there in the cold that he could not feel his legs. He leaned a minute on his spear, then got a footing with his back against the buttress and held his spear ready, not with the thrower but poised to use at short range.

The Gaal must be using ladders, for they were already inside the city over at the north side, he could tell by the noise. A spear sailed clear over the roofs, overshot with a thrower. The gate rattled again. In the old days they had no ladders and rams, they came not by thousands but in ragged tribes, cowardly barbarians, running south before the cold, not staying to live and die on their own Range as true men did. . . . There came one with a wide, white face and a red plume in his horn of pitch-smeared hair, running to open the gate from within. Wold took a step forward and said, "Stop there!" The Gaal looked around, and the old man drove his six-foot iron-headed spear into his enemy's side under the ribs, clear in. He was still trying to pull it back out of the shivering body when, behind him, the gate of the city began to split. That was a hideous sight, the wood splitting like rotten leather, the snout of a thick log poking through. Wold left his spear in the Gaal's belly and ran down the alley, heavily, stumbling, towards the House of his Kin. The peaked wooden roofs of the city were all on fire ahead of him.

CHAPTER EIGHT: *In The Alien City*

THE STRANGEST thing in all the strangeness of this house
was the painting on the wall of the big room downstairs.
When Agat had gone and the rooms were deathly still she
stood gazing at this picture till it became the world and she
the wall. And the world was a network: a deep network,
like interlacing branches in the woods, like inter-running
currents in water, silver, gray, black, shot through with
green and rose and a yellow like the sun. As one watched
their deep network one saw in it, among it, woven into it
and weaving it, little and great patterns and figures, beasts,
trees, grasses, men and women and other creatures, some
like farborns and some not; and strange shapes, boxes set
on round legs, birds, axes, silver spears and feathers of fire,
faces that were not faces, stones with wings and a tree
whose leaves were stars.

"What is that?" she asked the farborn woman whom
Agat had asked to look after her, his kinswoman; and she
in her way that was an effort to be kind replied, "A painting, a picture—your people make pictures, don't they?"

"Yes, a little. What is it telling of?"

"Of the other worlds and our home. You see the people
in it . . . It was painted long ago, in the first Year of our
exile, by one of the sons of Esmit."

"What is that?" Rolery pointed, from a respectful distance.

"A building—the Great Hall of the League on the world called Davenant."

"And that?"

"An erkar."

"I listen again," Rolery said politely—she was on her best manners at every moment now—but when Seiko Esmit seemed not to understand the formality, she asked, "What is an erkar?"

The farborn woman pushed out her lips a little and said indifferently, "A . . . thing to ride in, like a . . . well, you don't even use wheels, how can I tell you? You've seen our wheeled carts? Yes? Well, this was a cart to ride in, but it flew in the sky."

"Can your people make such cars now?" Rolery asked in pure wonderment, but Seiko took the question wrong. She replied with rancor, "No. How could we keep such skills here, when the Law commanded us not to rise above your level? For six hundred years your people have failed to learn the use of wheels!"

Desolate in this strange place, exiled from her people and now alone without Agat, Rolery was frightened of Seiko Esmit and of every person and every thing she met. But she would not be scorned by a jealous woman, an older woman. She said, "I ask to learn. But I think your people haven't been here for six hundred years."

"Six hundred home-years is ten Years here." After a moment Seiko Esmit went on, "You see, we don't know all about the erkars and many other things that used to belong to our people, because when our ancestors came here they were sworn to obey a law of the League, which forbade them to use many things different from the things the native people used. This was called Cultural Embargo. In time we would have taught you how to make things—like wheeled carts. But the Ship left. There were few of us here, and no word from the League, and we found many enemies among

67

your nations in those days. It was hard for us to keep the Law and also to keep what we had and knew. So perhaps we lost much skill and knowledge. We don't know."

"It was a strange law," Rolery murmured.

"It was made for your sakes—not ours," Seiko said in her hurried voice, in the hard distinct farborn accent like Agat's. "In the Canons of the League, which we study as children, it is written: *No Religion or Congruence shall be disseminated, no technique or theory shall be taught, no cultural set or pattern shall be exported, nor shall paraverbal speech be used with any non-Communicant highintelligence lifeform, or any Colonial Planet, until it be judged by the Area Council with the consent or the Plenum that such a planet be ready for Control or for Membership* . . . It means, you see, that we were to live exactly as you live. In so far as we do not, we have broken our own Law."

"It did us no harm," Rolery said. "And you not much good."

"You cannot judge us," Seiko said with that rancorous coldness; then controlling herself once more, "There's work to be done now. Will you come?"

Submissive, Rolery followed Seiko. But she glanced back at the painting as they left. It had a greater wholeness than any object she had ever seen. Its somber, silvery, unnerving complexity affected her somewhat as Agat's presence did; and when he was with her, she feared him, but nothing else. Nothing, no one.

The fighting men of Landin were gone. They had some hope, by guerilla attacks and ambushes, of harrying the Gaal on southward towards less aggressive victims. It was a bare hope, and the women were working to ready the town for siege. Seiko and Rolery reported to the Hall of the League on the great square, and there were assigned to help round up the herds of hann from the long fields south of town. Twenty women went together; each as she left the Hall was given a packet of bread and hann-milk curd, for they would be gone all day. As forage grew scant the herds had ranged far south between the beach and the coastal ridges. The women hiked about eight miles south and then beat back, zigzagging to and fro, collecting and driving the little, silent, shaggy beasts in greater and greater numbers.

Rolery saw the farborn women in a new light now. They had seemed delicate, childish, with their soft light clothes, their quick voices and quick minds. But here they were out in the ice-rimmed stubble of the hills, in furs and trousers like human women, driving the slow, shaggy herds into the north wind, working together, cleverly and with determination. They were wonderful with the beasts, seeming to lead rather than drive them, as if they had some mastery over them. They came up the road to the Sea Gate after the sun had set, a handful of women in a shaggy sea of trotting, high-haunched beasts. When Landin walls came in sight a woman lifted up her voice and sang. Rolery had never heard a voice play this game with pitch and time. It made her eyes blink and her throat ache, and her feet on the dark road kept the music's time. The singing went from voice to voice up and down the road; they sang about a lost home they had never known, about weaving cloth and sewing jewels on it, about warriors killed in war; there was a song about a girl who went mad for love and jumped into the sea, "O the waves they roll far out before the tide . . ." Sweet-voiced, making song out of sorrow, they came with the herds, twenty women walking in the windy dark. The tide was in, a soughing blackness over the dunes to their left. Torches on the high walls flared before them, making the city of exile an island of light.

All food in Landin was strictly rationed now. People ate communally in one of the great buildings around the square, or if they chose took their rations home to their houses. The women who had been herding were late. After a hasty dinner in the strange building called Thiatr, Rolery went with Seiko Esmit to the house of the woman

Alla Pasfal. She would rather have gone to Agat's empty house and been alone there, but she did whatever she was asked to do. She was no longer a girl, and no longer free. She was the wife of an an Alterran, and a prisoner on sufferance. For the first time in her life she obeyed.

No fire burned in the hearth, yet the high room was warm; lamps without wicks burned in glass cages on the wall. In this one house, as big as a whole Kinhouse of Tevar, one old woman lived by herself. How did they bear the loneliness? And how did they keep the warmth and light of summer inside the walls? And all Year long they lived in these houses, all their lives, never wandering, never living in tents out on the range, on the broad Summerlands, wandering . . . Rolery pulled her groggy head erect and stole a glance at the old one, Pasfal, to see if her sleepiness had been seen. It had. The old one saw everything; and she hated Rolery.

So did they all, the Alterrans, these farborn Elders. They hated her because they loved Jakob Agat with a jealous love; because he had taken her to wife; because she was human and they were not.

One of them was saying something about Tevar, something very strange that she did not believe. She looked down, but fright must have showed in her face, for one of the men, Dermat Alterra, stopped listening to the others and said, "Rolery, you didn't know that Tevar was lost?"

"I listen," she whispered.

"Our men were harrying the Gaal from the west all day," the farborn explained. "When the Gaal warriors attacked Tevar, we attacked their baggage-line and the camps their women were putting up east of the forest. That drew some of them off, and some of the Tevarans got out—but they and our men got scattered. Some of them are here now; we don't really know what the rest are doing, except it's a cold night and they're out there in the hills . . ."

Rolery sat silent. She was very tired, and did not understand. The Winter City was taken, destroyed. Could that be true? She had left her people; now her people were all dead, or homeless in the hills in the Winter night. She was left alone. The aliens talked and talked in their hard voices. For a while Rolery had an illusion, which she knew for an illusion, that there was a thin film of blood on her hands and wrists. She felt a little sick, but was not sleepy any longer; now and then she felt herself entering the outskirts, the first stage, of Absence for a minute. The bright, cold eyes of the old one, Pasfal the witch, stared at her. She could not move. There was nowhere to go. Everyone was dead.

Then there was a change. It was like a small light far off in darkness. She said aloud, though so softly only those nearest her heard, "Agat is coming here."

"Is he bespeaking you?" Alla Pasfal asked sharply.

Rolery gazed for a moment at the air beside the old woman she feared; she was not seeing her. "He's coming here," she repeated.

"He's probably not sending, Alla," said the one called Pilotson. "They're in steady rapport, to some degree."

"Nonsense, Huru."

"Why nonsense? He told us he sent to her very hard, on the beach, and got through; she must be a Natural. And that established a rapport. It's happened before."

"Between human couples, yes," the old woman said. "An untrained child can't receive or send a paraverbal message, Huru; a Natural is the rarest thing in the world. And this is a hilf, not a human!"

Rolery meanwhile had got up, slipped away from the circle and gone to the door. She opened it. Outside was empty darkness and the cold. She looked up the street, and in a moment could make out a man coming down it at a weary jogtrot. He came into the shaft of yellow light from the open door, and putting out his hand to catch hers, out of breath, said her name. His smile showed three front teeth gone; there was a blackened bandage around his head under his fur cap; he was grayish with fatigue and pain. He had been out in the hills since the Gaal had entered Aska-

71

tevar Range, three days and two nights ago. "Get me some water to drink," he told Rolery softly, and then came on into the light, while the others all gathered around him.

Rolery found the cooking-room and in it the metal reed with a flower on top which you turned to make water run out of the reed; Agat's house also had such a device. She saw no bowls or cups set out anywhere, so she caught the water in a hollow of the loose hem of her leather tunic, and brought it thus to her husband in the other room. He gravely drank from her tunic. The others stared and Pasfal said sharply, "There are cups in the cupboard." But she was a witch no longer; her malice fell like a spent arrow. Rolery knelt beside Agat and heard his voice.

CHAPTER NINE: *The Guerrillas*

THE WEATHER HAD warmed again after the first snow. There was sun, a little rain, northwest wind, light frost at night, much as it had been all the last moonphase of Autumn. Winter was not so different from what went before; it was a bit hard to believe the records of previous Years that told of ten-foot snowfalls, and whole moonphases when the ice never thawed. Maybe that came later. The problem now was the Gaal . . .

Paying very little attention to Agat's guerillas, though he had inflicted some nasty wounds on their army's flanks, the northerners had poured at a fast march down through Askatevar Range, encamped east of the forest, and now on the third day were assaulting the Winter City. They were not destroying it, however; they were obviously trying to save the granaries from the fire, and the herds, and perhaps the women. It was only the men they slaughtered. Perhaps, as reported, they were going to try to garrison the place with a few of their own men. Come Spring the Gaal returning from the south could march from town to town of an Empire.

It was not like the hilfs, Agat thought as he lay hidden under an immense fallen tree, waiting for his little army to take their positions for their own assault on Tevar. He had been in the open, fighting and hiding, two days and nights now. A cracked rib from the beating he had taken in the woods, though well bound up, hurt, and so did a shallow scalp-wound from a Gaal slingshot yesterday; but with immunity to infection wounds healed very fast, and Agat paid scant attention to anything less than a severed artery. Only a concussion had got him down at all. He was thirsty at the moment and a bit stiff, but his mind was pleasantly alert as he got this brief enforced rest. It wasn't like the hilfs, this planning ahead. Hilfs did not consider either time or space in the linear, imperialistic fashion of his own species. Time to them was a lantern lighting a step before, a step behind—the rest was indistinguishable dark. Time was this day, this one day of the immense Year. They had no historical vocabulary; there was merely today and "timepast." They looked ahead only to the next season at most. They did not look down over time but were in it as the lamp in the night, as the heart in the body. And so also with space: space to them was not a surface on which to draw boundaries but a range, a heartland, centered on the self and clan and tribe. Around the Range were areas that brightened as one approached them and dimmed as one departed; the farther, the fainter. But there were no lines, no limits. This planning ahead, this trying to keep hold of a conquered place across both space and time, was untypical; it showed—what? An autonomous change in a hilf culture-pattern, or an infection from the old northern colonies and forays of Man?

It would be the first time, Agat thought sardonically, that they ever learned an idea from us. Next we'll be catching their colds. And that'll kill us off; and our ideas might well kill them off . . .

There was in him a deep and mostly unconscious bitterness against the Tevarans, who had smashed his head and ribs, and broken their covenant; and whom he must now watch getting slaughtered in their stupid little mud city under his eyes. He had been helpless to fight against them, now he was almost helpless to fight for them. He detested them for forcing helplessness upon him.

At that moment—just as Rolery was starting back towards Landin behind the herds—there was a rustle in the dry leaf-dust in the hollow behind him. Before the sound had ceased he had his loaded dartgun trained on the hollow.

Explosives were forbidden by the Law of Cultural Embargo, which had become a basic ethos of the Exiles; but some native tribes, in the early Years of fighting, had used poisoned spears and darts. Freed by this from taboo, the doctors of Landin had developed some effective poisons which were still in the hunting-fighting repertory. There were stunners, paralyzers, slow and quick killers; this one was lethal and took five seconds to convulse the nervous system of a large animal, such as a Gaal. The mechanism of the dartgun was neat and simple, accurate within a little over fifty meters. "Come on out," Agat called to the silent hollow, and his still swollen lips stretched out in a grin. All things considered, he was ready to kill another hilf.

"Alterra?"

A hilf rose to his full height among the dead gray bushes of the hollow, his arms by his sides. It was Umaksuman.

"Hell!" Agat said, lowering his gun, but not all the way. Repressed violence shook him a moment with a spastic shudder.

"Alterra," the Tevaran said huskily, "in my father's tent we were friends."

"And afterwards—in the woods?"

The native stood there silent, a big, heavy figure, his fair hair filthy, his face clayey with hunger and exhaustion.

"I heard your voice, with the others. If you had to avenge your sister's honor, you could have done it one at a time." Agat's finger was still on the trigger; but when Umaksuman answered, his expression changed. He had not hoped for an answer.

"I was not with the others. I followed them, and stopped them. Five days ago I killed Ukwet, my nephew-brother, who led them. I have been in the hills since then."

Agat uncocked his gun and looked away.

"Come on up here," he said after a while. Only then did both of them realize that they had been standing up talking out loud, in these hills full of Gaal scouts. Agat gave a long noiseless laugh as Umaksuman slithered into the niche under the log with him. "Friend, enemy, what the hell," he said. "Here." He passed the hilf a hunk of bread from his wallet. "Rolery is my wife, since three days ago."

Silent, Umaksuman took the bread, and ate it as a hungry man eats.

"When they whistle from the left, over there, we're going to go in all together, heading for that breach in the walls at the north corner, and make a run through the town, to pick up any Tevarans we can. The Gaal are looking for us around the Bogs where we were this morning, not here. It's the only time we're going for the town. You want to come?"

Umaksuman nodded.

"Are you armed?"

Umaksuman lifted his ax. Side by side, not speaking, they crouched watching the burning roofs, the tangles and spurts of motion in the wrecked alleys of the little town on the hill facing them. A gray sky was closing off the sunlight; smoke was acrid on the wind.

Off to their left a whistle shrilled. The hillsides west and north of Tevar sprang alive with men, little scattered figures crouch-running down into the vale and up the slope, piling over the broken wall and into the wreckage and confusion of the town.

As the men of Landin met at the wall they joined into squads of five to twenty men, and these squads kept together, whether in attacking groups of Gaal looters with dartguns, bolos and knives, or in picking up whatever Tevaran women and children they found and making for the gate with them. They went so fast and sure that they might have rehearsed the raid; the Gaal, occupied in cleaning out the last resistance in the town, were taken off guard.

Agat and Umaksuman kept pace, and a group of eight or ten coalesced with them as they ran through the Stone-Pounding Square, then down a narrow tunnel-alley to a lesser square, and burst into one of the big Kinhouses. One after another leapt down the earthen stairway into the dark interior. White-faced men with red plumes twined in their horn-like hair came yelling and swinging axes, defending their loot. The dart from Agat's gun shot straight into the open mouth of one; he saw Umaksuman take the arm off a Gaal's shoulder as an axman lops a branch from a tree. Then there was silence. Women crouched in silence in the half-darkness. A baby bawled and bawled. "Come with us!" Agat shouted. Some of the women moved towards him, and seeing him, stopped.

Umaksuman loomed up beside him in the dim light from the doorway, heavy laden with some burden on his back. "Come, bring the children!" he roared, and at the sound of his known voice they all moved. Agat got them grouped at the stairs with his men strung out to protect them, then gave the word. They broke from the Kinhouse and made for the gate. No Gaal stopped their run—a queer bunch of women, children, men, led by Agat with a Gaal ax running cover for Umaksuman, who carried on his shoulders a great dangling burden, the old chief, his father Wold.

They made it out the gate, ran the gauntlet of a Gaal troop in the old tenting-place, and with other such flying squads of Landin men and refugees in front of them and behind them, scattered into the woods. The whole run through Tevar had taken about five minutes.

There was no safety in the forest. Gaal scouts and troops were scattered along the road to Landin. The refugees and rescuers fanned out singly and in pairs southward into the woods. Agat stayed with Umaksuman, who could not defend himself carrying the old man. They struggled through the underbrush. No enemy met them among the gray aisles and hummocks, the fallen trunks and tangled dead branches and mummied bushes. Somewhere far behind them a woman's voice screamed and screamed.

It took them a long time to work south and west in a half-circle through the forest, over the ridges and back north at last to Landin. When Umaksuman could not go any farther, Wold walked, but he could go only very slowly. When they came out of the trees at last they saw the lights of the City of Exile flaring far off in the windy dark above the sea. Half-dragging the old man, they struggled along the hillside and came to the Land Gate.

"Hilfs coming!" Guards sang out before they got within clear sight, spotting Umaksuman's fair hair. Then they saw Agat and the voices cried, "The Alterra, the Alterra!"

They came to meet him and brought him into the city, men who had fought beside him, taken his orders, saved his skin for these three days of guerilla-fighting in the woods and hills.

They had done what they could, four hundred of them against an enemy that swarmed like the vast migrations of the beasts—fifteen thousand men. Agat had guessed. Fifteen thousand warriors, between sixty or seventy thousand Gaal in all, with their tents and cookpots and travois and hann and fur rugs and axes and armlets and cradleboards and tinderboxes, all their scant belongings, and their fear of the Winter, and their hunger. He had seen Gall women in their encampments gathering the dead lichen off logs and eating it. It did not seem probable that the little City of Exile still stood, untouched by this flood of violence and hunger, with torches alight above its gates of iron and carved wood, and men to welcome him home.

Trying to tell the story of the last three days, he said, "We came around behind their line of march, yesterday afternoon." The words had no reality; neither had this warm room, the faces of men and women he had known all his life, listening to him. "The . . . the ground behind

them, where the whole migration had come down some of
the narrow valleys—it looked like the ground after a land-
slide. Raw dirt. Nothing. Everything trodden to dust, to
nothing . . ."

"How can they keep going? What do they eat?" Huru
muttered.

"The Winter stores in the cities they take. The land's all
stripped by now, the crops are in, the big game gone
south. They must loot every town on their course and live
off the hann-herds, or starve before they get out of the
snow-lands."

"Then they'll come here," one of the Alterrans said
quietly.

"I think so. Tomorrow or next day." This was true, but
it was not real either. He passed his hand over his face, feel-
ing the dirt and stiffness and the unhealed soreness of his
lips. He had felt he must come make his report to the gov-
ernment of his city, but now he was so tired that he could
not say anything more, and did not hear what they were
saying. He turned to Rolery, who knelt in silence beside
him. Not raising her amber eyes, she said very softly, "You
should go home, Alterra."

He had not thought of her all those endless hours of
fighting and running and shooting and hiding in the woods.
He had known her for two weeks; had talked with her at
any length perhaps three times; had lain with her once;
had taken her as his wife in the Hall of Law in the early
morning three days ago, and an hour later had left to go
with the guerillas. He knew nothing much about her, and
she was not even of his species. And in a couple of days
more they would probably both be dead. He gave his
noiseless laugh and put his hand gently on hers. "Yes, take
me home," he said. Silent, delicate, alien, she rose, and
waited for him as he took his leave of the others.

He had told her that Wold and Umaksuman, with about
two hundred more of her people, had escaped or been res-

cued from the violated Winter City and were now in refugee quarters in Landin. She had not asked to go to them.
As they went up the steep street together from Alla's
house to his, she asked, "Why did you enter Tevar to save
the people?"

"Why?" It seemed a strange question to him. "Because
they wouldn't save themselves."

"That's no reason, Alterra."

She seemed submissive, the shy native wife who did her
lord's will. Actually, he was learning, she was stubborn,
willful, and very proud. She spoke softly, but said exactly
what she meant.

"It is a reason, Rolery. You can't just sit there watching
the bastards kill off people slowly. Anyhow, I want to fight
—to fight back . . ."

"But your town: how do you feed these people you
brought here? If the Gaal lay siege, or afterwards, in Winter?"

"We have enough. Food's not our worry. All we need is
men."

He stumbled a little from weariness. But the clear cold
night had cleared his mind, and he felt the rising of a small
spring of joy that he had not felt for a long time. He had
some sense that this little relief, this lightness of spirit, was
given him by her presence. He had been responsible for
everything so long. She the stranger, the foreigner, of alien
blood and mind, did not share his power or his conscience
or his knowledge or his exile. She shared nothing at all with
him, but had met him and joined with him wholly and immediately across the gulf of their great difference: as if it
were that difference, the alienness between them, that let
them meet, and that in joining them together, freed them.

They entered his unlocked front door. No light burned
in the high narrow house of roughly dressed stone. It had
stood here for three Years, a hundred and eighty moonphases; his great-grandfather had been born in it, and his
grandfather, and his father, and himself. It was as familiar

to him as his own body. To enter it with her, the nomad woman whose only home would have been this tent or that on one hillside or another, or the teeming burrows under the snow, gave him a peculiar pleasure. He felt a tenderness towards her which he hardly knew how to express. Without intent he said her name not aloud but paraverbally. At once she turned to him in the darkness of the hall; in the darkness, she looked into his face. The house and city were silent around them. In his mind he heard her say his own name, like a whisper in the night, like a touch across the abyss.

"You bespoke me," he said aloud, unnerved, marveling. She said nothing but once more he heard in his mind, along his blood and nerves, her mind that reached out to him: *Agat, Agat . . .*

CHAPTER TEN: *The Old Chief*

THE OLD CHIEF was tough. He survived stroke, concussion, exhaustion, exposure, and disaster with intact will, and nearly intact intelligence.

Some things he did not understand, and others were not present to his mind at all times. He was if anything glad to be out of the stuffy darkness of the Kinhouse, where sitting by the fire had made such a woman of him; he was quite clear about that. He liked—he had always liked—this rock-founded, sunlit, windswept city of the farborns, built before anybody alive was born and still standing changeless in the same place. It was a much better built city than Tevar. About Tevar he was not always clear. Sometimes he remembered the yells, the burning roofs, the hacked and disemboweled corpses of his sons and grandsons. Sometimes he did not. The will to survive was very strong in him.

Other refugees trickled in, some of them from sacked Winter Cities to the north; in all there were now about three hundred of Wold's race in the farborns' town. It was so strange to be weak, to be few, to live on the charity of pariahs, that some of the Tevarans, particularly among the middle-aged men, could not take it. They sat in Absence, legs crossed, the pupils of their eyes shrunk to a dot, as if they had been rubbing themselves with gesin oil.

Some of the women, too, who had seen their men cut into gobbets in the streets and by the hearths of Tevar, or who had lost children, grieved themselves into sickness or Absence. But to Wold the collapse of the Tevaran world was only part of the collapse of his own life. Knowing that he was very far along the way to death, he looked with great benevolence on each day and on all younger men, human or farborn: they were the ones who had to keep fighting.

Sunlight shone now in the stone streets, bright on the painted housefronts, though there was a vague dirty smear along the sky above the dunes northward. In the great square, in front of the house called Thiatr where all the humans were quartered, Wold was hailed by a farborn. It took him a while to recognize Jaokob Agat. Then he cackled a bit and said, "Alterra! you used to be a handsome fellow. You look like a Pernmek shaman with his front teeth pulled. Where is . . . (he forgot her name) where's my kinswoman?"

"In my house, Eldest."

"This is shameful," Wold said. He did not care if he offended Agat. Agat was his lord and leader now, of course; but the fact remained that it was shameful to keep a mistress in one's own tent or house. Farborn or not, Agat should observe the fundamental decencies.

"She's my wife. Is that the shame?"

"I hear wrongly, my ears are old," Wold said, wary.

"She is my wife."

Wold looked up, meeting Agat's gaze straight on for the first time. Wold's eyes were dull yellow like the winter sun, and no white showed under the slanting lids. Agat's eyes were dark, iris and pupil dark, white-cornered in the dark face: strange eyes to meet the gaze of, unearthly.

Wold looked away. The great stone houses of the farborns stood all about him, clean and bright and ancient in the sunlight.

"I took a wife from you, Farborn," he said at last, "but I

never thought you'd take one from me . . . Wold's daughter married among the false-men, to bear no sons—"

"You've got no cause to mourn," the young farborn said unmoving, set as a rock. "I am your equal, Wold. In all but age. You had a farborn wife once. Now you've got a farborn son-in-law. If you wanted one you can swallow the other."

"It is hard," the old man said with dour simplicity. There was a pause. "We are not equals, Jakob Agat. My people are dead or broken. You are a chief, a lord. I am not. But I am a man, and you are not. What likeness between us?"

"At least no grudge, no hate," Agat said. still unmoving. Wold looked about him and at last, slowly, shrugged assent.

"Good, then we can die well together," the farborn said with his surprising laugh. You never knew when a farborn was going to laugh. "I think the Gaal will attack in a few hours, Eldest."

"In a few—?"

"Soon. When the sun's high maybe." They were standing by the empty arena. A light discus lay abandoned by their feet. Agat picked it up and without intent, boyishly, sailed it across the arena. Gazing where it fell he said, "There's about twenty of them to one of us. So if they get over the walls or through the gate . . . I'm sending all the Fall-born children and their mothers out to the Stack. With the drawbridges raised there's no way to take it, and it's got water and supplies to last five hundred people about a moonphase. There ought to be some men with the womenfolk. Will you choose three or four of your men, and the women with young children, and take them there?" They must have a chief. Does this plan seem good to you?"

"Yes. But I will stay here," the old man said.

"Very well, Eldest," Agat said without a flicker of protest, his harsh, scarred young face impassive. "Please choose the men to go with your women and children. They should go very soon. Kemper will take our group out."

"I'll go with them," Wold said in exactly the same tone, and Agat looked just a trifle disconcerted. So it was possible to disconcert him. But he agreed quietly. His deference to Wold was courteous pretense, of course—what reason had he to defer to a dying man who even among his own defeated tribe was no longer a chief?—but he stuck with it no matter how foolishly Wold replied. He was truly a rock. There were not many men like that. "My lord, my son, my like," the old man said with a grin, putting his hand on Agat's shoulder, "send me where you want me. I have no more use, all I can do is die. Your black rock looks like an evil place to die, but I'll do it there if you want . . ."

"Send a few men to stay with the women, anyway," Agat said, "good steady ones that can keep the women from panicking. I've got to go up to the Land Gate, Eldest. Will you come?"

Agat, lithe and quick, was off. Leaning on a farborn spear of bright metal, Wold made his way slowly up the streets and steps. But when he was only halfway he had to stop for breath, and then realized that he should turn back and send the young mothers and their brats out to the island, as Agat had asked. He turned and started down. When he saw how his feet shuffled on the stones he knew that he should obey Agat and go with the women to the black island, for he would only be in the way here.

The bright streets were empty except for an occasional farborn hurrying purposefully by. They were all ready or getting ready, at their posts and duties. If the clansmen of Tevar had been ready, if they had marched north to meet the Gaal, if they had looked ahead into a coming time the way Agat seemed to do . . . No wonder people called farborns witchmen. But then, it was Agat's fault that they had not marched. He had let a woman come between allies. If he, Wold, had known that the girl had ever spoken again to Agat, he would have had her killed behind the tents, and her body thrown into the sea, and Tevar might still be

85

standing . . . She came out of the door of a high stone house, and seeing Wold, stood still.

He noticed that though she had tied back her hair as married women did, she still wore leather tunic and breeches stamped with the trifoliate dayflower, clan-mark of his Kin.

They did not look into each other's eyes.

She did not speak. Wold said at last—for past was past, and he had called Agat "son"—"Do you go to the black island or stay here, kinswoman?"

"I stay here, Eldest."

"Agat sends me to the black island," he said, a little vague, shifting his stiff weight as he stood there in the cold sunlight, in his bloodstained furs, leaning on the spear.

"I think Agat fears the women won't go unless you lead them, you or Umaksuman. And Umaksuman leads our warriors, guarding the north wall."

She had lost all her lightness, her aimless, endearing insolence; she was urgent and gentle. All at once he recalled her vividly as a little child, the only little one in all the Summerlands, Shakatany's daughter, the summer-born. "So you are the Alterra's wife?" he said, and this idea coming on top of the memory of her as a wild, laughing child confused him again so he did not hear what she answered.

"Why don't all of us in the city go to the island, if it can't be taken?"

"Not enough water, Eldest. The Gaal would move into this city, and we would die on the rock."

He could see, across the roofs of the League Hall, a glimpse of the causeway. The tide was in; waves glinted beyond the black shoulder of the island fort.

"A house built upon sea-water is no house for men," he said heavily. "It's too close to the land under the sea . . . Listen now, there was a thing I meant to say to Arilia—to Agat. Wait. What was it, I've forgotten. I can't hear my mind . . ." He pondered, but nothing came. "Well, no matter. Old men's thoughts are like dust. Goodbye, daughter."

He went on, shuffling halt and ponderous across the Square to the Thiatr, where he ordered the young mothers to collect their children and come. Then he led his last foray—a flock of cowed women and little crying children, following him and the three younger men he chose to come with him, across the vasty dizzy air-road to the black and terrible house.

It was cold there, and silent. In the high vaults of the rooms there was no sound at all but the sound of the sea sucking and mouthing at the rocks below. His people huddled together all in one huge room. He wished old Kerly were there, she would have been a help, but she was lying dead in Tevar or in the forests. A couple of courageous women got the others going at last; they found grain to make bhanmeal, water to boil it, wood to boil the water. When the women and children of the farborns came with their guard of ten men, the Tevarans could offer them hot food. Now there were five or six hundred people in the fort, filling it up pretty full, so it echoed with voices and there were brats underfoot everywhere, almost like the women's side of a Kinhouse in the Winter City. But from the narrow windows, through the transparent rock that kept out the wind, one looked down and down to the water spouting on the rocks below, the waves smoking in the wind.

The wind was turning and the dirtiness in the northern sky had become a haze, so that around the little pale sun there hung a great pale circle: the snowcircle. That was it, that was what he had meant to tell Agat. It was going to snow. Not a shake of salt like last time, but snow, winter snow. The blizzard . . . The word he had not heard or said for so long made him feel strange. To die, then, he must return across the bleak, changeless landscape of his boyhood, he must reenter the white world of the storms.

He still stood at the window, but did not see the noisy water below. He was remembering Winter. A lot of good it would do the Gaal to have taken Tevar, and Landin too.

Tonight and tomorrow they could feast on hann and grain. But how far would they get, when the snow began to fall? The real snow, the blizzard that leveled the forests and filled the valleys; and the winds that followed, bitter cold. They would run when that enemy came down the roads at them! They had stayed North too long. Wold suddenly cackled out loud, and turned from the darkening window. He had out-lived his chiefdom, his sons, his use, and had to die here on a rock in the sea; but he had great allies, and great warriors served him—greater than Agat, or any man. Storm and Winter fought for him, and he would outlive his enemies.

He strode ponderously to the hearth, undid his gesin-pouch, dropped a tiny fragment on the coals and inhaled three deep breaths. After that he bellowed, "Well, women! Is the slop ready?" Meekly they served him; contentedly he ate.

CHAPTER ELEVEN: *The Siege of the City*

ALL THE FIRST DAY of the siege Rolery's job had been with those who kept the men on the walls and roofs supplied with lances—long, crude, unfinished slivers of holngrass weighing a couple of pounds, one end slashed to a long point. Well aimed, one would kill, and even from unskilled hands a rain of them was a good deterrent to a group of Gaal trying to raise a ladder against the curving landward wall. She had brought bundles of these lances up endless stairs, passed them up as one of a chain of passers on other stairs, run with them through the windy streets, and her hands still bristled with hair-thin, stinging splinters. But now since daybreak she had been hauling rocks for the *katapuls,* the rock-throwing-things like huge slingshots, which were set up inside the Land Gate. When the Gaal crowded up to the gate to use their rams, the big rocks whizzing and whacking down among tem scattered and rescattered them. But to feed the katapuls took an awful pile of rocks. Boys kept at work prising paving-stones up from the nearby streets, and her crew of women ran these eight or ten at a time on a little roundlegged box to the men working the katapuls. Eight women pulled together, harnessed to ropes. The heavy box with its dead load of stone would seem immovable, until at last as they all pulled its round legs would suddenly turn, and with it clattering and jolting behind, they would pull it uphill to the gate all in one straining rush, dump it, then stand panting a minute and wipe the hair out of their eyes, and drag the bucking, empty cart back for more. They had done this all morning. Rocks and ropes had blistered Rolery's hard hands raw. She had torn squares from her thin leather skirt and bound them on her palms with sandal-thongs; it helped, and others imitated her.

"I wish you hadn't forgotten how to make erkars," she shouted to Seiko Esmit once as they came clattering down the street at a run with the unwieldy cart jouncing behind them. Seiko did not answer; perhaps she did not hear. She kept at this grueling work—there seemed to be no soft ones among the farborns—but the strain they were under told on Seiko; she worked like one in a trance. Once as they neared the gate the Gaal began shooting fire-brands that fell smoking and smoldering on the stones and the tile roofs. Seiko had struggled in the ropes like a beast in a snare, cowering as the flamingo things shot over. "They go out, this city won't burn," Rolery said softly, but Seiko turning her unseeing face had said, "I'm afraid of fire, I'm afraid of fire . . ."

But when a young crossbowman up on the wall, struck in the face by a Gaal slingshot, had been thrown backwards off his narrow ledge and crashed down spread-eagled beside them, knocking over two of the harnessed women and spattering their skirts with his blood and brains, it had been Seiko that went to him and took that smashed head on her knees, whispering goodbye to the dead man. "That was your kinsman?" Rolery asked as Seiko resumed her harness and they went on. The Alterran woman said, "We are all kinsman in the City. He was Jonkendy Li—the youngest of the Council."

A young wrestler in the arena in the great square, shining with sweat and triumph, telling her to walk where she liked in his city. He was the first farborn that had spoken to her.

She had not seen Jakob Agat since the night before last, for each person, human and farborn, left in Landin had his job and place, and Agat's was everywhere, holding a city of fifteen hundred against a force of fifteen thousand. As the day wore on and weariness and hunger lowered her strength, she began to see him too sprawled out on bloody stones, down at the other main attack-point, the Sea Gate above the cliffs. Her crew stopped work to eat bread and dried fruit brought by a cheerful lad hauling a roundleg-cart of provisions; a serious little maiden lugging a skin of water gave them to drink. Rolery took heart. She was certain that they would all die, for she had seen, from the rooftops, the enemy blackening the hills: there was no end to them, they had hardly begun the siege yet. She was equally certain that Agat could not be killed, and that since he would live, she would live. What had death to do with him? He was life; her life. She sat on the cobbled street comfortable chewing hard bread. Mutilation, rape, torture and horror encompassed her within a stone's throw on all sides, but there she sat chewing her bread. So long as they fought back with all their strength, with all their heart, as they were doing, they were safe at least from fear.

But not long after came a very bad time. As they dragged their lumbering load towards the gate, the sound of the clattering cart and all sounds were drowned out by an incredible howling noise outside the gate, a roar like that of an earthquake, so deep and loud as to be felt in the bone, not heard. And the gate leaped on its iron hinges, shuddering. She saw Agat then, for a moment. He was running, leading a big group of archers and dartgunners up from the lower part of town, yelling orders to another group on the walls as he ran.

All the women scattered, ordered to take refuge in streets nearer the center of town. *Howw, howw, howw!* went the crowd-voice at the Land Gate, a noise so huge it seemed the hills themselves were making it, and would rise and shake the city off the cliffs into the sea. The wind was bitter cold. Her crew was scattered, all was confusion. She had no work to lay her hand to. It was getting dark. The day was not that old, it was not time yet for darkness. All at once she saw that she was in fact going to die, believed in her death; she stood still and cried out under her breath, there in the empty street between the high, empty houses.

On a side street a few boys were prising up stones and carrying them down to build up the barricades that had been built across the four streets that led into the main square, reinforcing the gates. She joined them, to keep warm, to keep doing something. They labored in silence, five or six of them, doing work too heavy for them.

"Snow," one of them said, pausing near her. She looked up from the stone she was pushing foot by foot down the street, and saw the white flakes whirling before her, falling thicker every moment. They all stood still. Now there was no wind, and the monstrous voice howling at the gate fell silent. Snow and darkness came together, bringing silence.

"Look at it," a boy's voice said in wonder. Already they could not see the end of the street. A feeble yellowish glimmer was the light from the League Hall, only a block away.

"We've got all Winter to look at the stuff," said another lad. "If we live that long. Come on! They must be passing out supper at the Hall."

"You coming?" the youngest one said to Rolery.

"My people are in the other house, Thiatr, I think."

"No, we're all eating in the Hall, to save work, Come on." The boys were shy, gruff, comradely. She went with them.

The night had come early; the day came late. She woke in Agat's house, beside him, and saw gray light on the gray walls, slits of dimness leaking through the shutters that hid the glass windows. Everything was still, entirely still. Inside the house and outside it there was no noise at all. How could a besieged city be so silent? But siege and Gaals seemed very far off, kept away by this strange daybreak hush. Here there was warmth, and Agat beside her lost in sleep. She lay very still.

Knocking downstairs, hammering at the door, voices. The charm broke; the best moment passed. They were calling Agat. She roused him, a hard job; at last, still blind with sleep, he got himself on his feet and opened window and shutter, letting in the light of day.

The third day of seige, the first of storm. Snow lay a foot deep in the streets and was still falling, ceaseless, sometimes thick and calm, mostly driving on a hard north wind. Everything was silenced and transformed by snow. Hills, forest, fields, all were gone; there was no sky. The near rooftops faded off into white. There was fallen snow, and falling snow, for a little ways, and then you could not see at all.

Westward, the tide drew back and back into the silent storm. The causeway curved out into void. The Stack could not be seen. No sky, no sea. Snow drove down over the dark cliffs, hiding the sands.

Agat latched shutter and window and turned to her. His face was still relaxed with sleep, his voice was hoarse. "They can't have gone," he muttered. For that was what they had been calling up to him from the street: "The Gaal have gone, they've pulled out, they're running south . . ."

There was no telling. From the walls of Landin nothing could be seen but the storm. But a little way farther into the storm there might be a thousand tents set up to weather it out; or there might be none.

A few scouts went over the walls on ropes. Three returned saying they had gone up the ridge to the forest and found no Gaal; but they had come back because they could not see even the city itself from a hundred yards off. One never came back. Captured, or lost in the storm?

The Alterrans met in the library of the Hall; as was customary, any citizen who wished came to hear and deliberate with them. The Council of the Alterrans was eight now, not ten. Jonkendy Li was dead and so was Haris, the youngest and the oldest. There were only seven present, for Pilotson was on guard duty. But the room was crowded with silent listeners.

"They're not gone . . . They're not close to the city . . . Some . . . some are . . ." Alla Pasfal spoke thickly, the pulse throbbed in her neck, her face was muddy gray. She was best trained of all the farborns at what they called mindhearing: she could hear men's thoughts farther than any other, and could listen to a mind that did not know she heard it.

That is forbidden, Agat had said long ago—a week ago? —and he had spoken against this attempt to find out if the Gaal were still encamped near Landin. "We've never broken that law," he said, "never in all the Exile." And he said, "We'll know where the Gaal are as soon as the snow lets up; meanwhile we'll keep watch."

But others did not agree with him, and they overrode his will. Rolery was confused and distressed when she saw him withdraw, accepting their choice. He had tried to explain to her why he must; he said he was not the chief of the city or the Council, that ten Alterrans were chosen and ruled together, but it all made no sense to Rolery. Either he was their leader or he was not; and if he was not, they were lost.

Now the old woman writhed, her eyes unseeing, and tried to speak in words her unspeakable half-glimpses into alien minds whose thoughts were in an alien speech, her brief inarticulate grasp of what another being's hands touched—"I hold—I hold—1-line—rope—" she stammered.

Rolery shivered in fear and distaste; Agat sat turned from Alla, withdrawn.

At last Alla was still, and sat for a long time with bowed head.

Seiko Esmit poured out for each of the seven Alterrans

and Rolery the tiny ceremonial cup of ti; each, barely touching it with his lips, passed it on to a fellow-citizen, and he to another till it was empty. Rolery looked fascinated at the bowl Agat gave to her, before she drank and passed it on. Blue, leaf-frail, it let the light pass through it like a jewel.

"The Gaal have gone," Alla Pasfal said aloud, raising her ravaged face. "They are on the move now, in some valley between two ranges—that came very clear."

"Giln Valley," one of the men murmured. "About ten kilos south from the Bogs."

"They are fleeing from the Winter. The walls of the city are safe."

"But the law is broken," Agat said, his hoarsened voice cutting across the murmur of hope and jubilation. "Walls can be mended. Well, we'll see . . ."

Rolery went with him down the stair case and through the vast Assembly Room, crowded now with trestles and tables, for the communal dining-hall was there under the golden clocks and the crystal patterns of planets circling their suns. "Let's go home," he said, and pulling on the big hooded furcoats that had been issued to everyone from the storerooms underneath the Old Hall, they went out together into the blinding wind in the Square. They had not gone ten steps when out of the blizzard a grotesque figure plastered with red-streaked white burst on them, shouting, "The Sea Gate, they're inside the walls, at the Sea Gate—"

Agat glanced once at Rolery and was gone into the storm. In a moment the clangor of metal on metal broke out from the tower overhead, booming, snow-muffled. They called that great noise the *bell,* and before the siege began had all learned its signals. Four, five strokes, then silence, then five again, and again: all men to the Sea Gate, the Sea Gate . . .

Rolery dragged the messenger out of the way, under the arcades of the League Hall, before men came bursting from the doors, coatless or struggling into their coats as they ran, armed and unarmed, pelting into the whirling snow, vanishing in it before they were across the Square.

No more came. She could hear some noise in the direction of the Sea Gate, seeming very remote through the sound of the wind and the hushing of the snow. The messenger leaned on her, in the shelter of the arcade. He was bleeding from a deep wound in his neck, and would have fallen if she had let him. She recognized his face; he was the Alterran called Pilotson, and she used his name to rouse him and keep him going as she tried to get him inside the building. He staggered with weakness and muttered as if still trying to deliver his message, "They broke in, they're inside the walls . . ."

CHAPTER TWELVE: *The Siege of the Square*

THE HIGH, narrow Sea Gate clashed to, the bolts shot home. The battle in the storm was over. But the men of the city turned and saw, over the red-stained drifts in the street and through the still-falling snow, shadows running.

They took up their dead and wounded hastily and returned to the Square. In this blizzard no watch could be kept against ladders, climbers; you could not see along the walls more than fifteen feet to either hand. A Gaal or a group of them had slipped in, right under the noses of the guards, and opened the Sea Gate to the assault. That assault had been driven out, but the next one could come anywhere, at any time, in greater force.

"I think," Umaksuman said, walking with Agat towards the barricade between the Thiatr and the College, "that most of the Gaal went on south today."

Agat nodded. "They must have. If they don't move on they starve. What we face now is an occupying force left behind to finish us off and live on our stores. How many do you think?"

"Not more than a thousand were there at the gate," the native said doubtfully. "But there may be more. And they'll all be inside the walls—There!" Umaksuman pointed to a quick cowering shape that the snow-curtains revealed for a moment halfway up the street. "You that way," the native muttered and vanished abruptly to the left. Agat circled the block from the right, and met Umaksuman in the street again. "No luck," he said.

"Luck," the Tevaran said briefly, and held up a bone-inlaid Gaal ax which he had not had a minute ago. Over their heads the bell of the Hall tower kept sending out its soft dull clanging through the snow: one, two—one, two—one, two—Retreat to the Square, to the Square . . . All who had fought at the Sea Gate, and those who had been patrolling the walls and the Land Gate, or asleep in their houses or trying to watch from the roofs, had come or were coming to the city's heart, the Square between the four great buildings. One by one they were let through the barricades. Imaksuman and Agat came along at last, knowing it was folly to stay out now in these streets where shadows ran. "Let's go, Alterra!" the native urged him, and Agat came, but reluctantly. It was hard to leave his city to the enemy.

The wind was down now. Sometimes, through the queer complex hush of the storm, people in the Square could hear glass shattering, the splintering of an ax against a door, up one of the streets that led off into the falling snow. Many of the houses had been left unlocked, open to the looters: they would find very little in them beyond shelter from the snow. Every scrap of food had been turned in to the Commons here in the Hall a week ago. The water-mains and the natural-gas mains to all buildings except the four around the Square had been shut off last night. The fountains of Landin stood dry, under their rings of icicles and burdens of snow. All stores and granaries were underground, in the vaults and cellars dug generations ago beneath the Old Hall and the League Hall. Empty, icy, lightless, the deserted houses stood, offering nothing to the invaders.

"They can live off our herds for a moonphase—even without feed for them, they'll slaughter the hann and dry the meat—" Dermat Alterra had met Agat at the very door of the League Hall, full of panic and reproach.

"They'll have to catch the hann first," Agat growled in reply.

"What do you mean?"

"I mean that we opened the byres a few minutes ago, while we were there at the Sea Gate, and let 'em go. Paol Herdsman was with me and he sent out a panic. They ran like a shot, right out into the blizzard."

"You let the hann go—the herds? What do we live on the rest of the winter—if the Gàal leave?"

"Did Paol mindsending to the hann panic you too, Dermat?" Agat fired at him. "D'you think we can't round up our own animals? What about our grain stores, hunting, snowcrop—what the devil's wrong with you!"

"Jakob," murmured Seiko Esmit, coming between him and the older man. He realized he had been yelling at Dermat, and tried to get hold of himself. But it was damned hard to come in from a bloody fight like that defense of the Sea Gate and have to cope with a case of male hysteria. His head ached violently; the scalp wound he had got in one of their raids on the Gaal camp still hurt, though it should have healed already; he had got off unhurt at the Sea Gate, but he was filthy with other men's blood. Against the high, unshuttered windows of the library the snow streaked and whispered. It was noon; it seemed dusk. Beneath the windows lay the Square with its well-guarded barricades. Beyond those lay the abandoned houses, the defenseless walls, the city of snow and shadows.

That day of their retreat to the Inner City, the fourth day of seige, they stayed inside their barricades; but already that night, when the snowfall thinned for a while, a reconnoitering party slipped out via the roofs of the College. The blizzard grew worse again around daybreak, or a second storm perhaps followed right on the first, and under cover of the snow and cold the men and boys of Landin played guerrilla in their own streets. They went out by twos or threes, prowling the streets and roofs and rooms, shadows among the shadows. They used knives, poisoned darts, bolos, arrows. They broke into their own homes and killed the Gaal who sheltered there, or were killed by them.

Having a good head for heights, Agat was one of the best at playing the game from roof to roof. Snow made the steep-pitched tiles pretty slippery, but the chance to pick off Gaal with darts was irresistible, and the chances of getting killed no higher than in other versions of the sport, streetcorner dodging or house-haunting.

The sixth day of seige, the fourth of storm: this day the snowfall was fine, sparse, wind-driven. Thermometers down in the basement Records Room of the old Hall, which they were using now as a hospital, read —4C. outside, and the anemometers showed gusts well over a hundred kmh. Outside it was terrible, the wind lashing that fine snow at one's face like gravel, whirling it in through the smashed glass of windows whose shutters had been torn off to build a campfire, drifting it across splintered floors. There was little warmth and little food anywhere in the city, except inside the four buildings around the Square. The Gaal huddled in empty rooms, burning mats and broken doors and shutters and chests in the middle of the floor, waiting out the storm. They had no provisions—what food there was had gone with the Southing. When the weather changed they would be able to hunt, and finish off the townsfolk, and thereafter live on the city's winter stores. But while the storm lasted, the attackers starved.

They held the causeway, if it was any good to them. Watchers in the League Tower had seen their one hesitant foray out to the Stack, which ended promptly in a rain of lances and a raised draw-bridge. Very few of them had been seen venturing on the low-tide beaches below the cliffs of Landin; probably they had seen the tide come roaring in, and had no idea how often and when it would come next, for they were inlanders. So the Stack was safe, and some of the trained paraverbalists in the city had been in touch with one or another of the men and women out on the island, enough to know they were getting on well, and to tell anxious fathers that there were no children sick. The Stack was all right. But the city was breached, invaded, occupied; more than a hundred of its people already killed in its defense, and the rest trapped in a few buildings. A city of snow, and shadows, and blood.

Jakob Agat crouched in a gray-walled room. It was empty except for a litter of torn felt matting and broken glass over which fine snow had sifted. The house was silent. There under the windows where the pallet had been, he and Rolery had slept one night; she had waked him in the morning. Crouching there, a housebreaker in his own house, he thought of Rolery with bitter tenderness. Once—it seemed far back in time, twelve days ago maybe—he had said in this same room thet he could not get on without her; and now he had no time day or night even to think of her. Then let me think of her now, at least think of her, he said ragefully to the silence; but all he could think was that she and he had been born at the wrong time. In the wrong season. You cannot begin a love in the beginning of the season of death.

Wind whistled peevishly at the broken windows. Agat shivered. He had been hot all day, when he was not freezing cold. The thermometer was still dropping, and a lot of the rooftop guerillas were having trouble with what the old men said was frostbite. He felt better if he kept moving. Thinking did no good. He started for the door out of a lifetime's habit, then getting hold of himself went softly to the window by which he had entered. In the ground-floor room of the house next door a group of Gaal were camped. He could see the back of one near the window. They were a fair people; their hair was darkened and made stiff with some kind of pitch or tar, but the bowed, muscular neck Agat looked down on was white. It was strange how little chance he had had actually to see his enemies. You shot from a distance, or struck and ran, or as at the Sea Gate fought too close and fast to look. He wondered if their eyes were yellowish or amber like those of the Tevarans; he had an impression that they were gray, instead. But this was no time to find out. He climbed up on the sill, swung out on the gable, and left his home via the roof.

His usual route back to the Square was blocked: the Gaal were beginning to play the rooftop game too. He lost all but one of his pursuers quickly enough, but that one, armed with a dart-blower, came right after him, leaping an eight-foot gap between two houses that had stopped the others. Agat had to drop down into an alley, pick himself up and run for it.

A guard on the Esmit Street barricade, watching for just such escapes, flung down a rope ladder to him, and he swarmed up it. Just as he reached the top a dart stung his right hand. He came sliding down inside the barricade, pulled the thing out and sucked the wound and spat. The Gaal did not poison their darts or arrows, but they picked up and used the ones the men of Landin shot at them, and some of these, of course, were poisoned. It was a rather neat demonstration of one reason for the canonical Law of Embargo. Agat had a very bad couple of minutes waiting for the first cramp to hit him; then decided he was lucky, and thereupon began to feel the pain of the messy little wound in his hand. His shooting hand, too.

Dinner was being dished out in the Assembly Hall, beneath the golden clocks. He had not eaten since daybreak. He was ravening hungry until he sat down at one of the tables with his bowl of hot bhan and salt meat; then he could not eat. He did not want to talk, either, but it was better than eating, so he talked with everyone who gathered around him, until the alarm rang out on the bell in the tower above them: another attack.

As usual, the assault moved from barricade to barricade; as usual it did not amount to much. Nobody could lead a prolonged attack in this bitter weather. What they were after in these shifting, twilight raids was the chance of slipping even one or two of their men over a momentarily un-guarded barricade into the Square, to open the massive iron doors at the back of Old Hall. As darkness came, the attackers melted away. The archers shooting from upper windows of the Old Hall and College held their fire and presently called down that the streets were clear. As usual, a few defenders had been hurt or killed: one crossbowman picked off at his window by an arrow from below, one boy who, climbing too high on the barricade to shoot down, had been hit in the belly with an iron-headed lance; several minor injuries. Every day a few more were killed or wounded and there were less to guard and fight. The subtraction of a few from too few . . .

Hot and shivering again, Agat came in from this action. Most of the men who had been eating when the alarm came went back and finished eating. Agat had no interest in food now except to avoid the smell of it. His scratched hand kept bleeding afresh whenever he used it, which gave him an excuse to go down to the Records Room, underneath Old Hall, to have the bonesetter tie it up for him.

It was a very large, low-ceilinged room, kept at even warmth and even soft light night and day, a good place to keep old instruments and charts and papers, and an equally good place to keep wounded men. They lay on improvised pallets on the felted floor, little islands of sleep and pain dotted about in the silence of the long room. Among them he saw his wife coming towards him, as he had hoped to see her. The sight, the real certain sight of her, did not rouse in him that bitter tenderness he felt when he thought about her: instead it simply gave him intense pleasure.

"Hullo, Rolery," he mumbled and turned away from her at once to Seiko and the bonesetter Wattock, asking how Huru Pilotson was. He did not know what to do with delight any more, it overcame him.

"His wound grows," Wattock said in a whisper. Agat

stared at him, then realized he was speaking of Pilotson. "Grows?" he repeated uncomprehending and went over to kneel at Pilotson's side.

Pilotson was looking up at him.

"How's it going, Huru?"

"You made a very bad mistake," the wounded man said.

They had known each other and been friends all their lives. Agat knew at once and unmistakably what would be on Pilotson's mind: his marriage. But he did not know what to answer. "It wouldn't have made much difference," he began finally, then stopped; he would not justify himself.

Pilotson said, "There aren't enough, there aren't enough."

Only then did Agat realize that his friend was out of his head. "It's all right, Huru!" he said so authoritatively that Pilotson after a moment sighed and shut his eyes, seeming to accept this blanket reassurance. Agat got up and rejoined Wattock. "Look, tie this up, will you, to stop the bleeding.—What's wrong with Pilotson?"

Rolery brought cloth and tape. Wattock bandaged Agat's hand with a couple of expert turns. "Alterra," he said, "I don't know. The Gaal must be using a poison our antidotes can't handle. I've tried 'em all. Pilotson Alterra isn't the only one. The wounds don't close; they swell up. Look at this boy here. It's the same thing." The boy, a street-guerilla of sixteen or so, was moaning and struggling like one in nightmare. The spear-wound in his thigh showed no bleeding, but red streaks ran from it under the skin, and the whole wound was strange to look at and very hot to the touch.

"You've tried antidotes?" Agat asked, looking away from the boy's tormented face.

"All of them. Alterra, what it reminds me of is the wound you got, early in Fall, from the *klois* you treed. Remember that? Perhaps they make some poison from the blood or glands of klois. Perhaps these wounds will go away as that did. Yes, that's the scar—When he was a young fellow like this one," Wattock explained to Seiko and Rolery, "he went up a tree after a klois, and the scratches it gave him didn't seem much, but they puffed up and got hot and made him sick. But in a few days it all went off again."

"This one won't get well," Rolery said very softly to Agat.

"Why do you say that?"

"I used to . . . to watch the medicine-woman of my clan. I learned a little . . . Those streaks, on his leg there, those are what they call death-paths."

"You know this poison, then, Rolery?"

"I don't think it's poison. Any deep wound can do it. Even a small wound that doesn't bleed, or that gets dirty. It's the evil of the weapon—"

"That is superstition," the old bonesetter said fiercely.

"We don't get the weapon-evil, Rolery," Agat told her, drawing her rather defensively away from the indignant old doctor. "We have an—"

"But the boy and Pilotson Alterra do have it! Look here —" She took him over to where one of the wounded Tevarans sat, a cheerful little middle-aged fellow, who willingly showed Agat the place where his left ear had been before an ax took it off. The wound was healing, but was puffed, hot, oozing . . .

Unconsciously Agat put his hand up to his own throbbing, untended scalp-wound.

Wattock had followed them. Glaring at the unoffending hilf, he said, "What the local hilfs call 'weapon-evil' is, of course, bacterial infection. You studied it in school, Alterra. As human beings are not susceptible to infection by any local bacterial or viral life-forms, the only harm we can suffer is damage to vital organs, exsanguination, or chemical poisoning, for which we have antidotes—"

"But the boy is dying, Elder," said Rolery in her soft, unyielding voice. "The wound was not washed out before it was sewed together—"

The old doctor went rigid with fury. "Get back among

your own kind and don't tell me how to care for humans—"

"That's enough," Agat said.

Silence.

"Rolery," Agat said, "if you can be spared here a while, I thought we might go . . ." He had been about to say, "go home." "To get some dinner, maybe," he finished vaguely.

She had not eaten; he sat with her in the Assembly Room, and ate a little. Then they put on their coats to cross the unlit, wind-whistling Square to the College building, where they shared a classroom with two other couples. The dormitories in Old Hall were more comfortable, but most of the married couples of which the wife had not gone out to the Stack preferred at least this semi-privacy, when they could have it. One woman was sound asleep behind a row of desks, bundled up in her coat. Tables had been up-ended to seal the broken windows from stones and darts and wind. Agat and his wife put their coats down on the unmatted floor for bedding. Before she let him sleep, Rolery gathered clean snow from a windowsill and washed the wounds in his hand and scalp with it. It hurt, and he protested, short-tempered with fatigue; but she said, "You are the Alterra—you don't get sick—but this will do no harm. No harm . . ."

CHAPTER THIRTEEN: *The Last Day*

IN HIS FEVERISH sleep, in the cold darkness of the dusty room, Agat spoke aloud sometimes, and once when she was asleep he called to her from his own sleep, reaching out across the unlit abyss, calling her name from farther and farther away. His voice broke her dreaming and she woke. It was still dark.

Morning came early: light shone in around the upturned tables, white streaks across the ceiling. The woman who had been there when they came in last night still slept on in exhaustion, but the other couple, who had slept on one of the writing-tables to avoid the drafts, roused up. Agat sat up, looked around, and said in his hoarse voice, with a stricken look, "The storm's over . . ." Sliding one of the tables aside a little they peered out and saw the world again: the trampled Square, snow-mounded barricades, great shuttered facades of the four buildings, snow-covered roofs beyond them, and a glimpse of the sea. A white and blue world, brilliantly clear, the shadows blue and every point touched by the early sunlight dazzling white.

It was very beautiful; but it was as if the walls that protected them had been torn down in the night.

Agat was thinking what she thought, for he said, "We'd better get on over to the Hall before they realize they can sit up on the rooftops and use us for target-practice."

"We can use the basement tunnels to get from one building to another," one of the others said. Agat nodded. "We will," he said. "But the barricades have got to be manned . . ."

Rolery procrastinated till the others had gone, then managed to persuade the impatient Agat to let her look at his head-wound again. It was improved or at least no worse. His face still showed the beating he had got from her kinsmen; her own hands were bruised from handling rocks and ropes, and full of sores that the cold had made worse. She rested her battered hands on his battered head and began to laugh. "Like two old warriors," she said. "O Jakob Agat, when we go to the country under the sea, will you have your front teeth back?"

He looked up at her, not understanding, and tried to smile, but failed.

"Maybe when a farborn dies he goes back to the stars—to the other worlds," she said, and ceased to smile.

"No," he said, getting up. "No, we stay right here. Come along, my wife."

For all the brilliant light from the sun and sky and snow, the air outside was so cold it hurt to breathe. They were hurrying across the square to the arcades of the League Hall when a noise behind them made them turn, Agat with his dartgun drawn, both ready to duck and run. A strange shrieking figure seemed to fly up over the barricade and crashed down headfirst inside it, not twenty feet from them: a Gaal, two lances bristling out between his ribs. Guards on the barricades stared and shouted, archers loaded their crossbows in haste, glancing up at a man who was yelling down at them from a shuttered window on the east side of the building above them. The dead Gaal lay face down in the bloody, trampled snow, in the blue shadow of the barricade.

One of the guards came running up to Agat, shouting "Alterra, it must be the signal for an attack—" Another man, bursting out of the door of the College, interrupted him, "No, I saw it, it was chasing him, that's why he was yelling like that—"

"Saw what? Did he attack like that all by himself?"

"He was running from it—trying to save his life! Didn't you see it, you on the barricade? No wonder he was yelling. White, runs like a man, with a neck like—God, like this, Alterra! It came around the corner after him, and then turned back."

"A snowghoul," Agat said, and turned for confirmation to Rolery. She had heard Wold's tales, and nodded. "White, and tall, and the head going from side to side . . ." She imitated Wold's grisly imitation, and the man who had seen the thing from the window cried, "That's it." Agat mounted the barricade to try and get a sight of the monster. She stayed below, looking down at the dead man, who had been so terrified that he had run on his enemy's lances to escape. She had not seen a Gaal up close, for no prisoners were taken, and her work had been underground with the wounded. The body was short and thin, rubbed with grease till the skin, whiter than her own, shone like fat meat; the greased hair was interbraided with red feathers. Ill-clothed, with a felt rag for a coat, the dead man lay sprawled in his abrupt death, face buried as if still hiding from the white beast that had hunted him. The girl stood motionless near him in the bright, icy shadow of the barricade.

"There!" she heard Agat shout, above her on the slanting, stepped inner face of the wall, built of paving-stones and rocks from the seacliffs. He came down to her, his eyes blazing, and hurried her off to the League Hall. "Saw it just for a second as it crossed Otake Street. It was running, it swung its head towards us. Do the things hunt in packs?"

She did not know; she only knew Wold's story of having killed a snowghoul single-handed, among last Winter's mythic snows. They brought the news and the question into the crowded refectory. Umaksuman said positively that snowghouls often ran in packs, but the farborns would not take a hilf's word, and had to go look in their *books*. The book they brought in said that snowghouls had been seen after the first storm of the Ninth Winter running in a pack of twelve to fifteen.

"How do the books say? They make no sound. It is like the mindspeech you speak to me?"

Agat looked at her. They were at one of the long tables in the Assembly Room, drinking the hot, thin grass-soup the farborns liked; ti, they called it.

"No—well, yes, a little. Listen, Rolery, I'll be going outside in a minute. You go back to the hospital. Don't mind Wattock's temper. He's an old man and he's tired. He knows a lot, though. Don't cross the Square if you have to go to another building, use the tunnels. Between the Gall archers and those creatures . . ." He gave a kind of laugh. "What next, I wonder?" he said.

"Jakob Agat, I wanted to ask you . . ."

In the short time she had known him, she had never learned for certain how many pieces his name came into, and which pieces she should use.

"I listen," he said gravely.

"Why is it that you don't speak mindspeech to the Gaal? Tell them to—to go. As you told me on the beach to run to the Stack. As your herdsman told the hann . . ."

"Men aren't hann," he said; and it occurred to her that he was the only one of them all that spoke of her people and his own and the Gaal all as men.

"The old one—Pasfal—she listened to the Gaal, when the big army was starting on south."

"Yes. People with the gift and the training can listen in, even at a distance, without the other mind's knowing it. That's a bit like what any person does in a crowd of people, he feels their fear or joy; there's more to mindhearing than that, but it's without words. But the mindspeech, and receiving mindspeech, is different. An untrained man, if you bespeak him, will shut his mind to it before he knows he's heard anything. Especially if what he hears isn't what he himself wants or believes. Non-Communicants have perfect defenses, usually. In fact to learn paraverbal communication is mainly to learn how to break down one's own defenses."

"But the animals hear?"

"To some extent. That's done without words again. Some people have that knack for projecting to animals. It's useful in herding and hunting, all right. Did you never hear that farborns were lucky hunters?"

"Yes, it's why they're called witches. But am I like a hann, then? I heard you."

"Yes. And you bespoke me—once, in my house—It happens sometimes between two people: there are no barriers, no defenses." He drained his cup and looked up broodingly at the pattern of sun and jeweled circling worlds on the long wall across the room. "When that happens," he said, "it's necessary that they love each other. Necessary . . . I can't send my fear or hate against the Gaal. They wouldn't hear. But if I turned it on you, I could kill you. And you me, Rolery . . ."

Then they came wanting him out in the square, and he must leave her. She went down to look after the Tevaran men in the hospital, which was her assigned job, and also to help the wounded farborn boy to die: a hard death that took all day. The old bonesetter let her take care of the boy. Wattock was bitter and rageful, seeing all his skill useless. "We humans don't die your foul death!" he stormed once. "The boy was born with some blood defect!" She did not care what he said. Neither did the boy, who died in pain, holding onto her hand.

New wounded were brought down into the big, quiet room, one or two at a time. Only by this did they know that there must be bitter fighting, up in the sunlight on the snow. Umaksuman was carried down, knocked unconscious by a Gaal slingshot. Great-limbed and stately he lay, and she looked at him with a dull pride: a warrior, a brother. She thought him near death, but after a while he sat up, shaking his head, and then stood up. "What place is this?"

he demanded, and she almost laughed when she answered. Wold's kin were hard to kill off. He told her that the Gaal were running an attack against all the barricades at once, a ceaseless push, like the great attack on the Land Gate when the whole force of them had tried to scale the walls on one another's shoulders. "They are stupid warriors," he said, rubbing the great lump over his ear. "If they sat up on the roofs around this Square for a week and shot at us with arrows, we wouldn't have men enough left to hold the barricades. All they know is to come running all at once, yelling . . ." He rubbed his head again, said, "What did they do with my spear?" and went back up to the fighting.

The dead were not brought down here, but laid in an open shed in the Square till they could be burned. If Agat had been killed, she would not know it. When bearers came with a new patient she looked up with a surge of hope: if it were Agat wounded, then he was not dead. But it was never him. She wondered if, when he was killed, he would cry out to her mind before he died; and if that cry would kill her.

Late in the unending day the old woman Alla Pasfal was carried down. With certain other old men and women of the farborns, she had demanded the dangerous job of bringing arms to the defenders of the barricades, which meant running across the Square with no shelter from the enemy's fire. A Gaal lance had pierced her throat from side to side. Wattock could do very little for her. A little, black, old woman, she lay dying among the young men. Caught by her gaze, Rolery went to her, a basin of bloody vomit in her hands. Hard, dark, and depthless as rock the old eyes gazed at her; and Rolery looked straight back, though it was not a thing her people did.

The bandaged throat rattled, the mouth twisted.

To break down one's own defenses . . .

"I listen!" Rolery said aloud, in the formal phrase of her people, in a shaking voice.

They will go, Alla Pasfal's voice, tired and faint, said in her mind: *They'll try to follow the others south. They fear us, the snowghouls, the houses and streets. They are afraid, they will go after this attack. Tell Jakob I can hear, I can hear them. Tell Jakob they will go—tomorrow—*

"I'll tell him," Rolery said, and broke into tears. Moveless, speechless, the dying woman stared at her with eyes like dark stones.

Rolery went back to her job, for the hurt men needed attention and Wattock had no other assistant. And what good would it do to go seek out Agat up there in the bloody snow and the noise and haste, to tell him, before he was killed, that a mad old woman dying had said they would survive?

She went on about her work with tears still running down her face. One of the farborns, badly wounded but eased by the wonderful medicine Wattock used, a little ball that, swallowed, made pain lessen or cease, asked her, "Why are you crying?" He asked it drowsily, curiosly, as one child might ask another. "I don't know," Rolery told him. "Go to sleep." But she did know, though vaguely, that she was crying because hope was intolerably painful, breaking through into the resignation in which she had lived for days; and pain, since she was only a woman, made her weep.

There was no way at all of knowing it down here, but the day must be ending, for Seiko Esmit came with hot food on a tray for her and Wattock and those of the wounded that could eat. She waited to take the bowls back, and Rolery said to her, "The old one, Pasfal Alterra, is dead."

Seiko only nodded. Her face was tight and strange. She said in a high voice, "They're shooting firebrands now, and throwing burning stuff down from the roofs. They can't break in so they're going to burn the buildings and the stores and then we all can starve together in the cold. If the Hall catches fire you'll be trapped down here. Burnt alive."

Rolery ate her food and said nothing. The hot bhan-meal

had been flavored with meat juice and chopped herbs. The farborns under siege were better cooks than her people in the midst of Autumn plenty. She finished up her bowl, and also the half-bowlful a wounded man left, and another scrap or two, and brought the tray back to Seiko, only wishing there had been more.

No one else came down for a long time. The men slept, and moaned in their sleep. It was warm; the heat of the gas-fires rose up through the gratings making it comfortable as a fire-warmed tent. Through the breathing of the men sometimes Rolery could hear the tick, tick, tick of the round-faced things on the walls, and they, and the glass cases pushed back against the wall, and the high rows of *books,* winked in gold and brown glimmerings in the soft, steady light of the gas-flares.

"Did you give him the analgesic?" Wattock whispered, and she shrugged yes, rising from beside one of the men. The old bonesetter looked half a Year older than he was, as he squatted down beside Rolery at a study table to cut bandages, of which they had run short. He was a very great doctor, in Rolery's eyes. To please him in his fatigue and discouragement she asked him, "Elder, if it's not the weapon-evil that makes a wound rot, what thing does?"

"Oh—creatures. Little beasts, too small to see. I could only show 'em to you with a special glass, like that one in the case over there. They live nearly everywhere; they're on the weapon, in the air, on the skin. If they get into the blood, the body resists 'em and the battle is what causes the swelling and all that. So the books say. It's nothing that ever concerned me as a doctor."

"Why don't the creatures bite farborns?"

"Because they don't like foreigners." Wattock snorted at his small joke. "We are foreign, you know. We can't even digest food here unless we take periodic doses of certain enzymoids. We have a chemical structure that's very slight-ly different from the local organic norm, and it shows up in the cytoplasm—You don't know what that is. Well, what it means is, we're made of slightly different stuff that you hilfs are."

"So that you're dark-skinned and we light?"

"No, that's unimportant. Totally superficial variations, color and eye-structure and all that. No, the difference is on a lower level, and is very small—one molecule in the hereditary chain," Wattock said with relish, warming to his lecture. "It causes no major divergence from the Common Hominid Type in you hilfs; so the first colonists wrote, and they knew. But it means that we can't interbreed with you; or digest local organic food without help; or react to your viruses. . . . Though as a matter of fact, this enzymoid business is a bit overdone. Part of the effort to do exactly as the First Generation did. Pure superstition, some of that. I've seen people come in from long hunting-trips, or the Atlantika refugees last Spring, who hadn't taken an enzymoid shot or pill for two or three moonphases, but weren't failing to digest. Life tends to adapt, after all." As he said this Wattock got a very odd expression, and stared at her. She felt guilty, since she had no idea what he had been explaining to her: none of the key words were words in her language. "Life what?" she inquired timidly.

"Adapts. Reacts. Changes! Given enough pressure, and enough generations, the favorable adaptation tends to prevail. . . . Would the solar radiation work in the long run towards a sort of local biochemical norm . . . all the still-births and miscarriages then would be overadaptations or maybe incompatibility between the mother and a normalized fetus . . ." Wattock stopped waving his scissors and bent to his work again, but in a moment he was looking up again in his unseeing, intense way and muttering, "Strange, strange, strange! . . . That would imply, you know, that cross-fertilization might take place."

"I listen again," Rollery murmured.

"That men and hilfs could breed together!"

This she understood at last, but did not understand whether he said it as a fact or a wish or a dread. "Elder, I am too stupid to hear you," she said.

"You understand him well enough," said a weak voice nearby: Pilotson Alterra, lying awake. "So you think we've finally turned into a drop in the bucket, Wattock?" Pilotson had raised up on his elbow. His dark eyes glittered in his gaunt, hot, dark face.

"If you and several of the others do have infected wounds, then the fact's got to be explained somehow."

"Damn adaptation then. Damn your crossbreeding and fertility!" the sick man said, and looked at Rolery. "So long as we've bred true we've been Man. Exiles, Alterrans, humans. Faithful to the knowledge and the Laws of Man. Now, if we can breed with the hilfs, the drop of our human blood will be lost before another Year's past. Diluted, thinned out to nothing. Nobody will set these instruments, or read these books. Jakob Agat's grandsons will sit pounding two rocks together and yelling, till the end of time . . . Damn you stupid barbarians, can't you leave men alone—alone!" He was shaking with fever and fury. Old Wattock, who had been fiddling with one of his little hollow darts, filling it up, now reached over in his smooth doctorly way and shot poor Pilotson in the forearm. "Lie down, Huru," he said, and with a puzzled expression the wounded man obeyed. "I don't care if I die of your filthy infections," he said in a thickening voice, "but your filthy brats, keep them away from here, keep 'em out of the . . . out of the City . . ."

"That'll hold him down a while," Wattock said, and sighed. He sat in silence while Rolery went on preparing bandages. She was deft and steady at such work. The old doctor watched her with a brooding face.

When she straightened up to ease her back she saw the old man too had fallen asleep, a dark pile of skin and bones hunched up in the corner behind the table. She worked on,

116

wondering if she had understood what he said, and if he had meant it: that she could bear Agat's son.

She had totally forgotten that Agat·might very well be dead already, for all she knew. She sat there among the sleep of wounded men, under the ruined city full of death, and brooded speechlessly on the chance of life.

CHAPTER FOURTEEN: *The First Day*

THE COLD gripped harder as night fell. Snow that had thawed in sunlight froze as slick ice. Concealed on nearby roofs or in attics, the Gaal shot over their pitch-tipped arrows that arched red and gold like birds of fire through the cold twilit air. The roofs of the four beleaguered buildings were of copper, the walls of stone; no fire caught. The attacks on the barricades ceased, no more arrows of iron or fire were shot. Standing up on the barricade, Jakob Agat saw the darkening streets slant off empty between dark houses.

At first the men in the Square waited for a night attack, for the Gaal were plainly desperate; but it grew colder, and still colder. At last Agat ordered that only the minimum watch be kept, and let most of the men go to get their wounds looked after, and get food and rest. If they were exhausted, so must the Gaal be, and they at least were clothed against this cold while the Gaal were not. Even desperation would not drive the northerners out into this awful, starlit clarity, in their scant rags of fur and felt. So the defenders slept, many at their posts, huddled in the halls and by the windows of warm buildings. And the besiegers, without food, pressed around campfires built in high stone rooms; and their dead lay stiff-limbed in the ice-crusted snow below the barricades.

Agat wanted no sleep. He could not go inside the buildings, leaving the Square where all day long they had fought for their lives, and which now lay so still under the Winter constellations. The Tree; and the Arrow; and the Track of five stars; and the Snowstar itself, fiery above the eastern roofs: the stars of Winter. They burned like crystals in the profound, cold blackness overhead.

He knew this was the last night—his own last night, or his city's, or the last night of battle—which one, he did not know. As the hours wore on, and the Snowstar rose higher, and utter silence held the Square and the streets around it, a kind of exultation got hold of him. They slept, all the enemies within these city walls, and it was as if he alone waked; as if the city belonged, with all its sleepers and all its dead, to him alone. This was his night.

He would not spend it locked in a trap within a trap. With a word to the sleepy guard, he mounted the Esmit Street barricade and swung himself down on the other side. "Alterra!" someone called after him in a hoarse whisper; he only turned and gestured that they keep a rope ready for him to get back up on, and went on, right up the middle of the street. He had a conviction of his invulnerability with which it would be bad luck to argue. He accepted it, and walked up the dark street among his enemies as if he were taking a stroll after dinner.

He passed his house but did not turn aside. Stars eclipsed behind the black roof-peaks and reappeared, their reflections glittering in the ice underfoot. Near the upper end of town the street narrowed and turned a little between houses that had been deserted since before Agat was born, and then opened out suddenly into the little square under the Land Gate. The catapults still stood there, partly wrecked and dismantled for firewood by the Gaal, each with a heap of stones beside it. The high gates themselves had been opened at one point, but were bolted again now and frozen fast. Agat climbed up the steps beside one of the gate-towers to a post on the wall; he remembered looking down from that post, just before the snow began, on the whole battle-force of the Gaal, a roaring tide of men like the seatide down on the beach. If they had had more ladders it would have all been over with that day . . . Now nothing moved; nothing made any sound. Snow, silence, starlight over the slope and the dead, ice-laden trees that crowned it.

He looked back westward, over the whole City of Exile; a little clutter of roofs dropping down away from his high post to the wall over the seacliff. Above that handful of stone the stars moved slowly westward. Agat sat motionless, cold even in his clothing of leather and heavy furs, whistling a jig-tune very softly.

Finally he felt the day's weariness catching up with him, and descended from his perch. The steps were icy. He slipped on the next to bottom step, caught himself from falling by grabbing the rough stone of the wall, and then still staggering looked up at some movement that had caught his eyes across the little square.

In the black gulf of a street opening between two house-walls, something white moved, a slight swaying motion like a wave seen in the dark. Agat stared, puzzled. Then it came out into the vague gray of the starlight: a tall, thin, white figure running towards him very quickly as a man runs, the head on the long, curving neck swaying a little from side to side. As it came it made a little wheezing, chirping sound.

His dartgun had been in his hand all along, but his hand was stiff from yesterday's wound, and the glove hampered him: he shot and the dart struck, but the creature was already on him, the short clawed forearms reaching out, the head stuck forward with its weaving, swaying motion, a round toothed mouth gaping open. He threw himself down right against its legs in an effort to trip it and escape the first lunge of that snapping mouth, but it was quicker than he. Even as he went down it turned and caught at him, and he felt the claws on the weak-looking little arms tear through the leather of his coat and clothing, and felt himself pinned down. A terrible strength bent his head back, baring his throat; and he saw the stars whirl in the sky far up above him, and go out.

And then he was trying to pull himself up on hands and knees, on the icy stones beside a great, reeking bulk of white fur that twitched and trembled. Five seconds it took the poison on the darttip to act; it had almost been a second too long. The round mouth still snapped open and shut, the legs with their flat, splayed, snowshoe feet pumped as if the snowghoul were still running. Snowghouls hunt in packs, Agat's memory said suddenly, as he stood trying to get his breath and nerve back. Snowghouls hunt in packs . . . He reloaded his gun clumsily but methodically, and, with it held ready, started back down Esmit Street; not running lest he slip on the ice, but not strolling, either. The street was still empty, and serene, and very long.

But as he neared the barricade, he was whistling again.

He was sound asleep in the room in the College when young Shevik, their best archer, came to rouse him up, whispering urgently, "Come on, Alterra, come on, wake up, you've got to come . . ." Rolery had not come in during the night; the others who shared the room were all still asleep.

"What is it, what's wrong?" Agat mumbled, on his feet and struggling into his torn coat already.

"Come on to the Tower," was all Shevik said.

Agat followed him, at first with docility, then, waking up fully, with beginning understanding. They crossed the Square, gray in the first bleak light, ran up the circular stairs of the League Tower, and looked out over the city. The Land Gate was open.

The Gaal were gathered inside it, and going out of it. It was hard to see them in the half-light before sunrise; there were between a thousand and two thousand of them, the men watching with Agat guessed, but it was hard to tell. They were only shadowy blots of motion under the walls and on the snow. They strung out from the Gate in knots and groups, one after another disappearing under the walls and then reappearing farther away on the hillside, going at a jogtrot in a long irregular line, going south. Before they had gone far the dim light and the folds of the hill hid them; but before Agat stopped watching the east had grown bright, and a cold radiance reached halfway up the sky.

The houses and the steep streets of the city lay very quiet in the morning light.

Somebody began to ring the bell, right over their heads in the tower there, a steady rapid clamor and clangor of bronze on bronze, bewildering. Hands over their ears, the men in the tower came running down, meeting other men and women halfway. They laughed and they shouted after Agat and caught at him, but he ran on down the rocking stairs, the insistent jubilation of the bell still hammering at him, and into the League Hall. In the big, crowded, noisy room where golden suns swam on the walls and the years and Years were told on golden dials, he searched for the alien, the stranger, his wife. He finally found her, and taking her hands he said, "They're gone, they're gone, they're gone . . ."

Then he turned and roared it with all the force of his lungs at everybody—"They're gone!"

They were all roaring at him and at one another, laughing and crying. After a minute he said to Rolery, "Come on with me—out to the Stack." Restless, exultant, bewildered, he wanted to be on the move, to get out into the city and make sure it was their own again. No one else had left the Square yet, and as they crossed the west barricade Agat drew his dartgun. "I had an adventure last night," he said to Rolery, and she, looking at the gaping rent in his coat, said, "I know."

"I killed it."

"A snowghoul?"

"Right."

"Alone?"

"Yes. Both of us, fortunately."

The solemn look on her face as she hurried along beside him made him laugh out loud with pleasure.

They came out onto the causeway, running out in the icy wind between the bright sky and the dark, foam-laced water.

The news of course had already been given, by the bell and by mindspeech, and the drawbridge of the Stack was lowered as soon as Agat set foot on the bridge. Men and women and little sleepy, fur-bundled children came running to meet them, with more shouts, questions, and embraces.

Behind the women of Landin, the women of Tevar hung back, afraid and unrejoicing. Agat saw Rolery going to one of these, a young woman with wild hair and dirt-smudged face. Most of them had hacked their hair short and looked unkempt and filthy, even the few hilf men who had stayed out at the Stack. A little disgusted by this grimy spot on his bright morning of victory, Agat spoke to Umaksuman, who had come out to gather his tribesmen together. They stood on the drawbridge, under the sheer wall of the black fort. Hilf men and women had collected around Umaksuman, and Agat lifted up his voice so they all could hear. "The Men of Tevar kept our walls side by side with the Men of Landin. They are welcome to stay with us or to go, to live with us or leave us, as they please. The gates of my city are open to you, all Winter long. You are free to go out them, but welcome within them!"

"I hear," the native said, bowing his fair head.

"But where's the Eldest, Wold? I wanted to tell him—"

Then Agat saw the ash-smeared faces and ragged heads with a new eye. They were in mourning. In understanding that he remembered his own dead, his friends, his kinsmen; and the arrogance of triumph went out of him.

Umaksuman said, "The Eldest of my Kin went under

123

the sea with his sons who died in Tevar. Yesterday he went. They were building the dawn-fire when they heard the bell and saw the Gaal going south."

"I would watch this fire," Agat said, asking Umaksuman's permission. The Tevaran hesitated, but an older man beside him said firmly, "Wold's daughter is this one's wife: he has clan right."

So they let him come, with Rolery and all that were left of her people, to a high terrace outside a gallery on the seaward side of the Stack. There on a pyre of broken wood the body of the old man lay, age-deformed and powerful, wrapped in a red cloth, death's color. A young child set the torch and the fire burnt red and yellow, shaking the air, paled by the cold early light of the sun. The tide was drawing out, grinding and thundering at the rocks below the sheer black walls. East over the hills of Askatevar Range and west over the sea the sky was clear, but northward a bluish dusk brooded: Winter.

Five thousand nights of Winter, five thousand days of it: the rest of their youth and maybe the rest of their lives.

Against that distant, bluish darkness in the north, no triumph showed up at all. The Gaal seemed a little scurry of vermin, gone already, fleeing before the true enemy, the true lord, the white lord of the Storms. Agat stood by Rolery in front of the sinking death-fire, in the high sea-beleaguered fort, and it seemed to him then that the old man's death and the young man's victory were the same thing. Neither grief nor pride had so much truth in them as did joy, the joy that trembled in the cold wind between sky and sea, bright and brief as fire. This was his fort, his city, his world; these were his people. He was no exile here.

"Come," he said to Rolery as the fire sank down to ashes, "come, let's go home."

SAMUEL R. DELANY

*04594	Babel 17 $1.50
19683	Einstein Intersection $1.50
20571	The Ballad of Beta2/Empire Star $1.25
22642	The Fall of the Towers $1.95
39021	Jewels of Aptor 75¢

ROGER ZELAZNY

37468	Isle of the Dead $1.50
16704	The Dream Master $1.50
24903	Four For Tomorrow $1.50
80694	This Immortal $1.50

PHILIP JOSÉ FARMER

05360	Behind the Walls of Terra $1.25
78652	The Stone God Awakens $1.25
89238	The Wind Whales of Ishmael $1.25

CLIFFORD D. SIMAK

10624	**City** $1.75
77220	**So Bright the Vision** $1.50
81002	**Time and Again** $1.75
82442	**The Trouble With Tycho** $1.50

Ursula K. Le Guin

10703	**City of Illusion**	$1.75
47803	**Left Hand of Darkness**	$1.95
66953	**Planet of Exile**	$1.25
73293	**Rocannon's World**	$1.50

Available wherever paperbacks are sold or use this coupon.